Dear Flora and Bear,
May you know that
you are unique and
special!
Enjoy!
Elaine Slade
x

Copyright © 2021 Slade Books.

www.elainesladebooks.com

elaine@elainesladebooks.com

ISBN: 978-1-8384003-0-9

A CIP catalogue record for this book is available from the British Library.

BOZ PUBLICATIONS

First published by Boz Publications Ltd 2021

Boz Publications Ltd.

71-75 Shelton Street, Covent Garden, London WC2H 9JQ

office@bozpublications.com - www.bozpublications.com

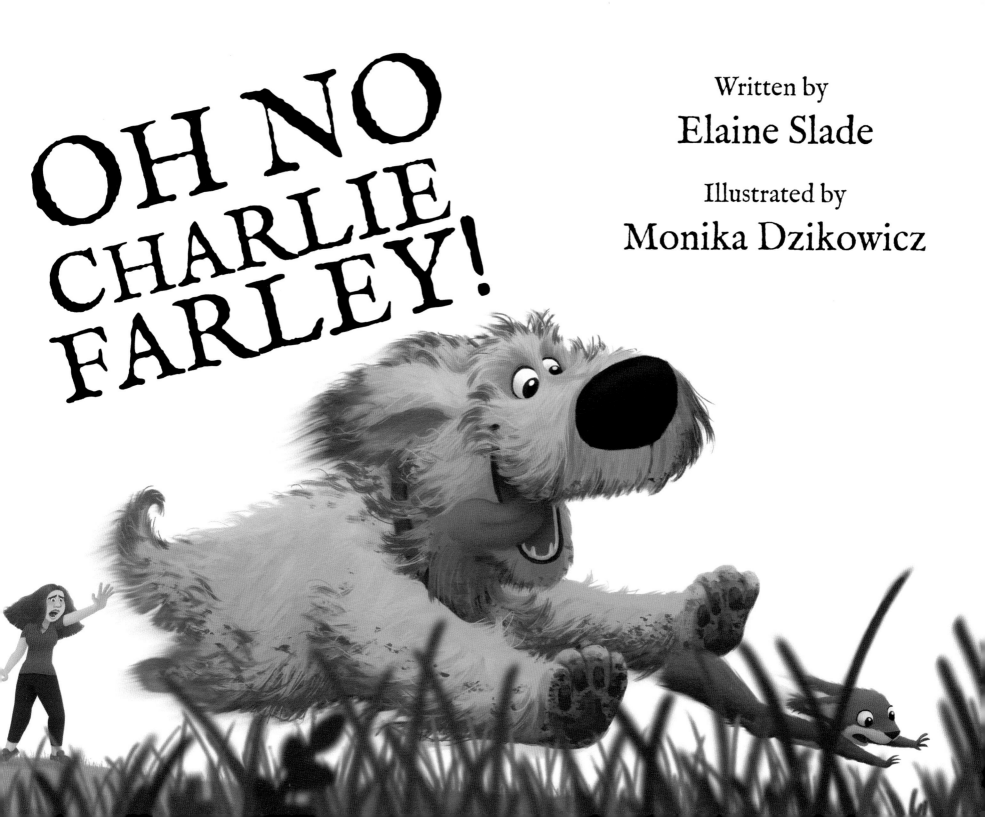

OH NO CHARLIE FARLEY!

Written by
Elaine Slade

Illustrated by
Monika Dzikowicz

Jasper was a Goldendoodle.

Part Retriever,
mostly Poodle.

Behold dog owners beam and clap,
he really was a handsome chap.

Charlie Farley was a...

...Goldendoodle?

Mostly Retriever,
where's the Poodle?

Watch dog owners scowl and frown,
he really was a scruffy clown.

Jasper's fur always neat and white,

whilst Charlie Farley's remained a messy sight.

Jasper loved water, he always found
the cleanest puddles on the ground.

Charlie Farley loved water,
he always found the muddiest
mire for miles around.

Jasper loved to fetch and chase.
Always elegant, full of grace.

Charlie Farley loved to fetch and fling,
he really was the clumsiest thing.

OH NO

Jasper's fur was easy to brush,
standing there without a fuss.

Charlie Farley's tufts were
impossible to groom,
causing his owner
to splutter and fume.

Charlie Farley was so down,
everywhere he looked
he saw a frown.

Why wasn't HE
like Jasper?

OH NO!
What's this?!

"Jasper, save my little pup,
this thorny bush has tangled him up".

Jasper tried his hardest to be brave,
but the little pup he could not save.

What can be done to solve this disaster?

"*Charlie Farley, here's a job for you!*"
said Jasper.

Charlie Farley tumbles into the brambles,
searches round then out he scrambles.

Puppy safely in his gentle grasp,
making all the dog owners gasp.

Charlie places pup on the ground,
his owners SO grateful he's been found.

Puppy runs to the little girl;
happy Charlie gives a twirl.

OH YES
CHARLIE
FARLEY!!!

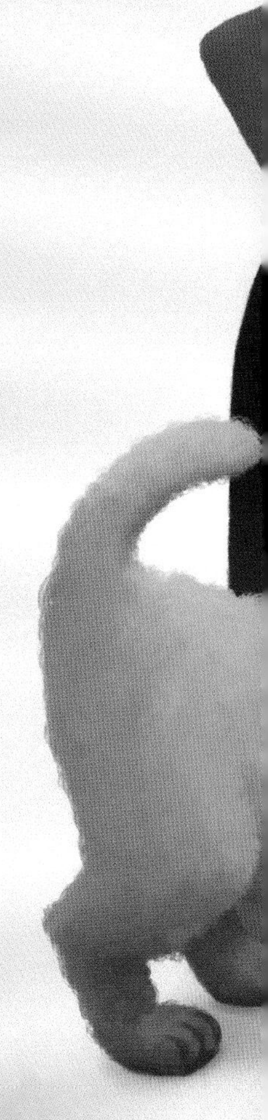

Charlie Farley was Jasper's brother.
Although they didn't look like each other,
both were special in their own unique way.

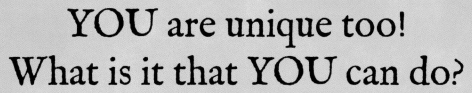

I am good at _____.

Meet the REAL
Charlie Farley and Jasper.

OH NO CHARLIE FARLEY
is based on real life dogs
within Elaine's family.

These books are inspired
by their unique characters.

LOOK!

CHARLIE FARLEY'S NEXT EXCITING ADVENTURE.

Charlie Farley out of sight.
Under the blanket, crouched in fright.
BANG, his-ss-ss, crackle, BOOM!
Fireworks meant doom and gloom.

DON'T BE SCARED, CHARLIE FARLEY!

Jasper loved to fetch and chase, Always elegant, full of grace.
Charlie Farley love to fetch and fling, he really was the clumsiest thing.

OH NO CHARLIE FARLEY!

First, Monika starts with a simple sketch, to represent Elaine's words into images. It's very messy, keeps it fun and easy to change if she finds a better way to show this scene.

How Charlie Farley came to life.

Next, she draws the page in more detail and colours! Before, the characters didn't look like anyone, but now they must be Charlie and his friends. Can you see if anything else changed in this scene?

Jasper loved to fetch and chase.
Always elegant, full of grace.

Charlie Farley love to fetch and fling, he really was the clumsiest thing.

OH NO   CHARLIE FARLEY!

Jasper loved to fetch and chase.
Always elegant, full of grace.

Charlie Farley love to fetch and fling,
he really was the clumsiest thing.

OH NO   CHARLIE FARLEY!

Now you can clearly see what
was missing in the previous scene.
In this page, Elaine wanted the puppy
to be partially lost in the bushes.
So, Monika drew him right back
in with plenty of trees around.

Although it looks like Monika is taking
a step back, this is a technical stage.
You can now impress your parents
and teachers with words like
perspective, form and composition.
Monika is making sure this scene makes
you feel like you are there with Charlie.

Jasper loved to fetch and chase.
Always elegant, full of grace.

Charlie Farley loved to fetch and fling,
he really was the clumsiest thing.

OH NO   CHARLIE FARLEY!

Jasper loved to fetch and chase.
Always elegant, full of grace.

Charlie Farley loved to fetch and fling,
he really was the clumsiest thing.

OH NO   CHARLIE FARLEY!

And finally, Monika paints and paints
and paints until she feels like Charlie is
jumping off the page right into her arms!
She hopes you feel it too!

CHARLIE'S ACTIVITY GUIDE!
- Helping children to internalise and understand their value and uniqueness. -

Complete the page 'What is it that you can do?' together.
Encourage your child/ren to describe themselves in positive terms and to talk about their abilities.

Using two other animals e.g. cats, rabbits create a story using the same storyline, you could use two animal puppets.

Make Charlie Farley and Jasper out of playdough, then role play the story together OR act out the story together.
Talk about how the characters feel as you go through it.

Look at any words in the story that your child might not have understood e.g. mire, elegant, splutter.
Explain them or look together at a Dictionary or on the internet to find out the meaning.

Draw a picture of Charlie Farley and Jasper showing their differences. For example, Jasper in a clean puddle
and Charlie Farley in a muddy puddle. Talk about why they got different reactions from the dog owners.

On a rainy day get your wellies on and splash in the puddles; discuss whether you and your child prefer
clean puddles like Jasper or muddy puddles like Charlie Farley.

Make up a different ending to the story; how could Charlie Farley find out in another way that he is special too?

Practice throwing and catching a ball like Jasper, but don't try and catch squirrels like Charlie Farley!

Talk together about what a dog needs to keep them healthy and content and write a fact sheet
on how to look after a dog.

Can you spot the rhyming words in each section of the text?
Try other rhyming activities such as how many words rhyme with *dog*.

Draw a picture of a forest and draw a little squirrel hidden in the picture somewhere;
ask someone to spot the squirrel.

Count how many dogs there are in the story.

JASPER'S MESSAGE TO PARENTS AND TEACHERS.

Before reading the book, look at the cover:

Who do you think this story might be about?
What does the blurb tell us on the back of the book?

Whilst reading the book:

Can you find the little squirrel as we turn over each page?
Where is the story happening? How can you tell?
Encourage your child/ren to take the lead in calling out 'Oh No Charlie Farley!' and then even louder 'Oh Yes Charlie Farley!'
'Everywhere he looked he saw a frown.' How did Charlie Farley feel? Why?
'Jasper save my little pup.' What is happening on this page? What is the little girl thinking? How can you tell?
'Jasper tried his hardest to be brave.' How does Jasper feel? Why?
What do you think will happen next after Jasper gives up?
'Charlie Farley, here's a job for you!' Why did Jasper suggest that this was a job for Charlie Farley?
How does Charlie Farley feel at the end of the story? Why?

After reading the book:

Who are the main characters?
Which dog would you like to own, Jasper or Charlie Farley? Why?
Can you spot where the puppy runs off into the bush in the story?
Which part of the story did you like best? Why was that?

Ideas to help explore uniqueness through the story:

What was the difference between Jasper and Charlie Farley?
Did it matter that the dogs were different?
Have you ever felt like Charlie Farley did when people seemed to like Jasper more?
If your child wants to, chat together about their uniqueness and what makes their sibling or friend special too.
Talk about what to do next time if they feel someone else is better than them or is getting more attention.

Elaine Slade - Author

Elaine is a former Deputy Head who loves exploring a good story and inspiring children, including her family (four daughters, two granddaughters), to love reading. She is passionate about raising children's self-esteem and affirming their uniqueness. Elaine enjoys a challenge like Charlie Farley; she has trekked up to 4000m in the Himalayas and lived in Romania for three years.

www.elainesladebooks.com

Monika Dzikowicz - Illustrator

Monika, just like Charlie Farley, spent most of her childhood covered in mud; frolicking in nature; and looking up to her cool, older sister. When she grew up she embraced her uniqueness and became an illustrator who strives to visualise stories, which empower people and teach them emotional intelligence.

www.monikadzikowicz.com

To my UNIQUE granddaughters, Zoë and Phoebe, each special in their own way and best friends with Charlie Farley and Jasper.

Elaine Slade

Thanks to my husband for supporting me in being the best version of myself, and to my sister for showing me how to be strong and generous.

Monika Dzikowicz

THE MEON VALLEY RAILWAY
A Construction & Social History
Part 1: BUILDING THE LINE

Compiled by Kevin Robertson

ISBN 978-1-906419-47-9

First published in 2011 by Kevin Robertson under the **NOODLE BOOKS** imprint
PO Box 279, Corhampton, SOUTHAMPTON. SO32 3ZX

www.noodlebooks.co.uk

Printed in England by Ian Allan Printing.

1. Front cover - *Construction at what is probably the approach to West Meon tunnel. The track is of course temporary as laid by the contractor for his own use and will be replaced later by standard LSWR fittings. Whilst we can be certain the view is from the days of the construction of the Meon Valley, the location has resulted in much debate. Sufficient width for double track yet in a cutting. This narrows the search down to the stations or tunnel approaches. None of the stations was situated within a cutting and which thus leaves it as being one of the two tunnels. Privett is less likely and it is reasonable then to assume that this is the initial approach to the north end of West Meon tunnel.*

2. Frontispiece - *Looking south at what will become the site of the station at West Meon. Contractors wagons stand on the position of the later up line, with, in the distance, a temporary cut through destined to become the bridge carrying Station Road.*

Rear cover - *Painted image in preparation by Craig Tilley.*

Note - Each image is numbered consecutively throughout this book. Where known, the locations of these images are shown on the map on Page 8.

INTRODUCTION

This is a book like no other, so far as a railway in the South of England is concerned. Indeed, apart from the renowned Newton Collection illustrating the construction of the Great Central Railway, images of railway building are either restricted to the occasional view taken by a local photographer, a chance inclusion of building work secondary to the main subject, or perhaps a few localised images showing a railway complete and around the time of opening. This omission is both sad and in many respects surprising.

True, the building of the trunk lines of the 1840s or earlier, was before the development of photography proper, but it must be said there were still numerous lines laid out subsequent to this time and where any illustrative record is either in the criteria previously referred to or missing altogether. For whatever reason, it seems neither the railway company nor the contractor involved saw photography as a desirability: clearly the value of the image in a portfolio and thus a potential means of procurement of future work was not yet realised.

Enter then the Meon Valley Railway in East Hampshire, built between 1898 and 1903. At this time, as in decades past and indeed for some time to come, the role of human muscle power was paramount in its construction, supplemented it must be said by contractors railway engines, wagons, horses, carts and the then still relatively modern invention of the 'steam navvy' - 'steam shovel' or 'steam excavator' would be a more accurate description.

For some six years it was men alone who were primarily responsible for the work. Covering part of this time, certainly from 1899 onwards, the spiritual and moral needs of these navvies, their families and the younger 'nippers', was in the care of the redoubtable Missionary David Smith[1]. During the period David Smith was present, he collected an album of photographs of the work. More than a century later that album is a prized family heirloom in the hands of his grandson, David Foster-Smith, and it is with the latter's generous assistance that this book has been made possible.

What is the most remarkable facet is that David Foster-Smith may not in any way be regarded as a railway enthusiast. He is though enthused over his ancestry, and so with album in hand made a trip, some years ago, to Privett, in an attempt to try and identify certain of the locations illustrated in the album. At this stage it should be stated that the original is a most fragile and consequently delicate volume. Few locations are annotated by name, Privett Church being one of the very few and whilst the album contains something in excess of 150 photographs, these have also faded much over the years. Whether they were taken by David Smith or simply collected by him, we cannot know. The inclusion of several totally unrelated subjects is a matter for debate, although others, particularly a number of ecclesiastical images from the local area are perhaps more easily explained. The local gentry also feature from time to time: was this even where David Smith was acting on behalf of his 'flock' attempting to obtain assistance

for the needy, or possibly even act as a mediator in times of conflict?

David Foster-Smith's own visit to Privett in the 1980s might so easily have led to nothing. Coincidentally though, there was a young girl delivering newspapers in the vicinity and who was approached to enquire if anyone locally might know anything of the former railway. That remark put David Foster-Smith in contact with Ray Stone of West Meon. Ray Stone's knowledge of the local area is considerable and so between them it was possible to identify several other locations. Bear in mind however, this was already some 80 years since the photographs had been taken. Eight decades in which foliage and vegetation had grown rife, added to which since closure of the line in 1955, areas had already been returned to their former state. Some locations can only be guessed at.

This was also around the time Ray Stone was contemplating his own 'Meon Valley Railway' book [2] which, when it appeared, contained a limited selection of the images from the David Smith album.

There matters might have rested, except that is for an approach by the present compiler to both Ray Stone and subsequently David Foster-Smith to see more. The results are shown on the following pages. Modern technology allowing new life to be breathed into the old [3]. What you will see are the best, the most interesting, and containing, I hope, the most variety. Others, of peripheral content, such as described earlier, have been deliberately omitted, not least for reason of space.

With the assistance of several friends, notably Denis Tillman, it has been possible to identify several 'new' locations, although in consequence a number of additional questions have now arisen as well. Some of these came from the obvious - when it was eventually realised the album (there are no contents or index) represented progress down the valley from north to south and not necessarily in date order of construction.

It is hoped this book will find a wider audience than the railway market alone; it certainly deserves this. As alluded to at the start, it is probably unique, and whilst I would dearly love to be proven wrong, I doubt very much if another similar collection will ever be found.

Living in the Meon Valley myself, I regularly exercise my Labrador on a stretch of the former railway now turned into a footpath. In so doing, the mind often wanders back to the time that very spot may have been visited by the actual photographer.

Kevin Robertson, Corhampton 2010

1 - A brief outline of the truly fascinating life of David Smith and how he came to become a Railway Missionary is given on pages 4 to 7.
2 - Kingfisher Railway Publications, later reprinted by Runpast Publications.
3 - With grateful thanks to the photographic wizardry of Bruce Murray.

A MISSIONARY MAN

DAVID SMITH was born in Newhaven on 10 August 1866, the tenth of twelve children of parents William and Mary Smith. Two of his siblings had died as infants.

His Father, William Smith, was a 'Blacksmith Journeyman' who travelled the country widely for his work. In consequence William Smith's children are recorded as being born at locations as far apart as Bradford, Yorkshire; South Shields, County Durham; Beeley, Derbyshire; Penarth and Portcawl, Glamorgan; Newhaven, East Sussex; and Bristol.

By 1876 the family were living in Shirehampton, Bristol, where William Smith was the Chief Blacksmith for the New Avonmouth Dock then under construction. David Smith by now aged 10, was also already working, "...my job was to collect and carry heavy tools up to the Smithy for sharpening." The following year the family moved to No. 1 Queen Street, Avonmouth. At this time David's eldest brother, also William, opened his own Smithy at Kings Weston, Bristol where David is known to have assisted in the work.

The family moved to Cardiff in 1883 where William Smith (Snr) had secured the contract for all the Blacksmith work at the new Roath Dock. In consequence the various businesses set up at Avonmouth were sold and on 28 April 1883, David together with the youngest sister Rose then aged about 12, set out on the steam packet 'The Druid' from Bristol. William Smith (Snr) was reported as having died just over a year later in July 1884, aged 58.

It appears not all the family may have travelled to Cardiff in 1883, although his now widowed mother and other members of the family were later resident there in two rented rooms, for which they paid 4/- weekly. David Smith would appear to have been the main bread-winner at this stage, supplemented by his mother making shirts for the men on the New Dock for 2/6d each.

In 1887 the family moved to Barry, where work on the Dock was under way. Despite also hoping to finish learning his own trade here, David Smith instead found himself filling wagons as a Navvy for a paltry 4¼d per hour. These low wages also compelled the family to take in lodgers.

Two years later in 1889, David Smith joined two of his brothers at Runcorn, working on the Manchester Ship Canal. His Mother also joined them, although she was now suffering poor health and died in March 1890, aged 61.

David Smith recalls the difficult times at Runcorn, "...we had several hard times of struggle, as the works were often stopped (through industrial stoppages or financial implications), and as no money was coming in, we got very much behind."

It was at Runcorn that David and his youngest sister Rose began to take an interest in the Navvy Mission; indeed Rose would later marry a man with similar ideals. For his own part, David Smith was heavily influenced in the path his own future would take by the Rev. Robert Grimston, Vicar at Runcorn Parish Church, although it would be Mrs Elizabeth Garnett (1839-1921) [1] the redoubtable welfare reformer, who was ultimately responsible for persuading David Smith to become a missionary. [2]

David Smith's own notes record, "...it was here that I should become acquainted with Matilda Kate Foster, who as well as living virtually next door to us at Runcorn was to become my wife and a co-worker at the Mission." David and

3. David Smith, the Navvy - seated bottom row far right. Pictured at Barry Dock sometime between 1887 and 1889.

Matilda married in April 1890, three of their five children shown as having been born in the same area. It was also around 1890 that David Smith became a missionary.

By May 1899 and the birth of their fourth child, David and Matilda were at Catcleugh in Northumberland, and it in this area that the first of what are the three albums of photographs showing the construction work taking place in the area where he himself was a missionary commences. Whether the various images were taken by him, commissioned by him, or simply sourced from various photographers cannot be confirmed. Possibly a combination of all three. Very roughly they follow in date order, and besides the reservoir at Catcleugh and obviously the Meon Valley railway, there are images of various public works contracts as well as social gather-

ings, the local gentry, mission work and occasionally the results of accidents. An astonishing total in excess of 400 photographs. To be fair, not all are of interest outside the family, whilst others are certainly not of publishable quality. We also know David Smith had lantern slides made from a number of these images which he appears to have used in lectures: possibly illustrating his past work when sent to his next assignment - or should we even say 'Parish'?

The fact he had himself once been a navvy may well have aided his credibility with the actual navvy men and their families. He was employed in his missionary work by the Industrial Christian Fellowship and paid a wage (stipend) equal to the average pay of a navvy on the site. The Missionary's wife was also expected to help the children and women on the navvy site: this involved schooling, conse-

6. *The house at No. 20 Bailey Green, (Stocks Lane) Privett, circa 1901, with most of Smith family members present. As wife of the Missionary, Mrs. Smith was expected to assist the navvy families, even though the Smith household was not immediately adjacent to the actual site of the navvy camp: located half to one mile distant.*

by the LSWR, that the route might not turn out to be as viable after all. Accordingly, there seems to have been little urgency to complete the work, a later source quoting from un-named contemporary records implies the work should have been expected to have occupied just three years. Did it even lie moribund for a time? [5]

We now have to question the actual images available. Most of those seen are, as mentioned, from the collection of David Smith's grandson, David Foster-Smith. All too often family records, photographs, paperwork and other heirlooms are of little interest to successive generations who have had no personal contact with the individuals depicted or items concerned. It is then sad to come across in antique and second hand shops and even at boot fairs, boxes of Victorian, Edwardian and even later photographs without attributable names, discarded by a family who have no interest in their ancestry. Fortunately this was not the case here, the result being a priceless archive so far as the social and railway historian is concerned.

But in dealing with the Meon Valley photographs there are obvious gaps. There are for example, no views of the route being surveyed prior to construction, of any celebratory 'Cutting of the First Sod' - if indeed there was any celebra-

quently we know that Kate (Matilda) became involved in sewing classes to help make ends meet. Accommodation was provided for the family. Whereas, however, a navvy having sixpence or a shilling in his pocket might be expected to spend this on drink, David Smith was recalled by his wife as always willing to give away to a good cause any money he might have upon him. As a result, it was recalled by his wife that life was not easy for the Smith family.

Why David Smith should be sent to Hampshire we cannot be certain. One guess is it was in consequence of the fatal accident[3] that occurred to Navvy George Brown in Privett Tunnel in January 1899. Whatever, the family took up residence at 20 Bailey Green, Privett and where the accompanying photograph was recorded in 1901. It was also at Privett, on 28 October 1901, that the youngest child, Nellie Vida Smith was born.[4]

From various records we know the actual construction of the Meon Valley line was beset with difficulties. Labour shortage - possibly due to men serving in the campaigns associated with the second Boar War (1899 - 1902), the weather, difficulties with the terrain and, it appears, a realisation and consequent lack of urgency

tion, no known views of the construction between Butts Junction and Farringdon ('Faringdon' - sic), nothing (that can be identified) of Tisted or Droxford, nothing of the line complete or of the Board of Trade Inspection or opening, and as has been said before, no dates, confirmation of locations or indeed an index.

That is not in any way intended to criticise, perhaps instead we may learn and instead recognise that the actual images represent what was in place when David Smith arrived and, in the main, the area where he 'ministered'. Had there even been a Navvy Missionary before him, if so who and where? Perhaps David Smith was responsible for just one area and there were others. Records do not exist to confirm or deny any of this so far as the Meon Valley was concerned, but certainly we know that elsewhere some of the larger public works contracts did have more than one missionary present.

It is now that the contents of some of the other albums play a part, for there are illustrations of mission huts and work associated with various army camps on Salisbury Plain circa 1901, followed by further railway scenes near Bristol and later more reservoir construction. What this leads to is a conclusion that David Smith left

Privett sometime after 1901 - certainly he was at Chipping Sodbury, Gloucestershire, by 1903. At this stage the Meon Valley line was far from complete, but as born out by the comments made earlier, with no urgency by the LSWR as to its completion. Yes, there are images of the tunnels at Privett and West Meon and the site of what later became the famed West Meon Viaduct but nothing of the latter's construction.

Some of these omissions may be filled, in part, from other photographs of the construction era pooled from separate sources. Where such items have been used this is annotated accordingly. In the ensuing 100 plus years since the time of construction and opening no other similar record to cover the period pre- and post-David Smith's time at Privett has been discovered, leading to the conclusion that it was indeed he who either took or commissioned most of the images himself.

Subsequent to 1903 there are in the albums only a few images of various locations. These include several scenes of street gatherings, including a particularly poignant view of young men listening to David Smith at the Birmingham 'Bull Ring' where he would stand on a soap box and argue his case before a sometimes heckling crowd: his theme was of course the Navvy Missionary Society. (We know the family came to Birmingham in 1906 and left in 1926 to live in Luton.) This Birmingham image is dated June 1914. What makes it so moving is that just a few weeks later in August 1914 WW-1 erupted and with it the call for the flower of youth to prostrate themselves on the battlefield. This wartime connection is mentioned as it may not be widely known that whilst the navvy as a breed had quietly disappeared by the 1930s, mainly as a result of mechanisation, navvies were being employed by the military in France in WW-1, mainly to dig trenches, their considerable abilities to shift 'muck', as any form of earth was referred to, well recognised. With them again went the missionaries. (We know from family records that David Smith made a Will following his commission as a Chaplain [sic] in anticipation of being sent to France during WW-1. In the event this tour did not materialise.)

Aside then from the obvious legacy of his descendents and his work as a missionary, his other legacy is this photographic collection. I doubt if he could ever have imagined the cultural importance it represents.

David Smith died at his home 'Penpole', Luton, Befordshire, on 13 April 1932, aged 65 years, he had been married to Kate for 42 years. She would survive him by a further 17 years.

7. Typical of some of the non railway images from the Meon Valley album is this wonderful period view of the F. Andrews village shop at Privett and associated transport. The actual location is thought to be at Staple Ash and included the village Post Office. (The collection includes another, undated image, showing a wedding of the Andrews family, presumably recorded during the time David Smith was in the area.)

1 - The work of the Navvy Mission Society (- later the Industrial Christian fellowship), was begun in Yorkshire in 1877 by the Rev. Lewis Moule Evans, later succeeded by Elizabeth Garnett. Mrs Garnett and another contemporary lady with similar ideals, Katie Marsh, have been referred to by Dick Sullivan in his book 'Navvyman' as "...the navvy's arch-friends." Miss Marsh never married and though Mrs Garnett obviously did, her husband died on their honeymoon soon after her wedding. Both were daughters of Anglican Clergymen.

2 - Although throughout this text the term 'Missionary' is used, neither David Smith nor his colleagues in similar Mission work were ordained Ministers and a more accurate description would have been that of a 'Lay-Preacher'. However, they preached from 'Mission Huts' provided by the Navvy Mission Society and in consequence were thus referred to as 'Missionaries'. It is only in more recent times that the same term has come to be associated also exclusively with a (usually) Christian individual attempting to convert others in far flung continents.

3 - Unattributed papers in the South Western Circle Portfolio imply there were several fatal accidents to men on the Meon Valley line. Known details of these incidents are included in the text. The lack of information on David Smith between 1890 and 1899 other than the birth of his children recorded on their respective birth certificates, implies he would have undergone training somewhere. Dick Sullivan in 'Navvyman' places him at some time as a 'Missioner' on the Great Central running the 'Good Samaritan' for tramp navvies at Bulwell, south of Nottingham. Maybe this even instigated David's interest in retaining photographic records? David Foster-Smith also reports on his own research of 2010 which revealed another Missioner had replaced David Smith at the Catcleugh Reservoir (Yorkshire) consequent upon the latter's move to Hampshire: which suggests missioners were moved around, probably doing a two or three year stint (posting) at each site. As mentioned, we know David Smith was still at Privett in late 1901, subsequently moving to Chipping Sodbury in 1902/03.

4 - Later in this work are illustrations of the opening of the Navvy Mission at Privett in 1899: perhaps Mr. Smith was busy from the moment he arrived! (A similar mission hut was provided at West Meon.) Denis Tillman's excellent pictorial work *MEON VALLEY REVISITED* (Kestrel Railway Books) has, on page 5, an image purporting to be of a navvy missionary and men stated as being at Droxford. The missionary so depicted is certainly not David Smith.

5 - This lack of urgency contradicts the comments of Sir Charles Scotter of the LSWR, reported in the 'Hampshire Telegraph & Sussex Chronicle' of Saturday 30 January 1897. At that time, and no doubt in an effort to convince Parliament of the intent of the LSWR, Scotter stated, ",,,the Company intended to make the line quickly." It is a matter of much regret that no records of the contractor involved. Robert T. Relf and Son of Plymouth, have been located. (The spelling Relfe is also used in some contemporary records.)

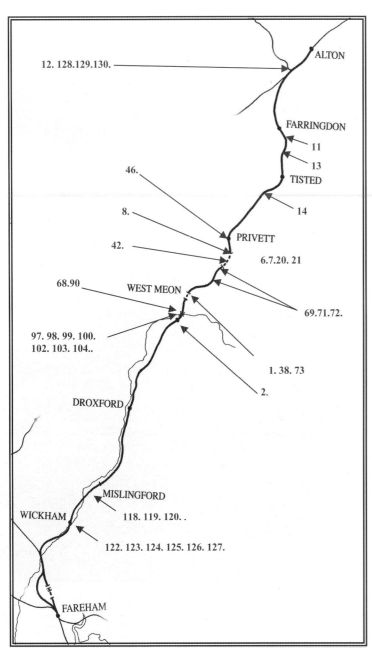

ALTON

12. 128.129.130.

FARRINGDON

11

13

TISTED

46.

14

8.

PRIVETT

42.

6.7.20. 21

WEST MEON

68.90

69.71.72.

97. 98. 99. 100.
102. 103. 104..

1. 38. 73

2.

DROXFORD

MISLINGFORD

WICKHAM

118. 119. 120. .

122. 123. 124. 125. 126. 127.

FAREHAM

The route of the Meon Valley Railway. Figures in red refer to the location, where known, an image appearing within this book was taken. Map courtesy of Denis Tillman.

Building the new line would have involved work starting simultaneously at several points. Without however, the benefit of any records of construction, actual detail must be conjecture, based upon reasonable logic and subsequent information gleaned from newspaper reports and the accompanying photographs.

We know for example, that by 1901 at the latest, possibly as early as 1899, a physical connection existed at what would later be Butts Junction, south east of Alton (the point of divergence of the Light Railway to Basingstoke), and it was via this link that materials would have been taken as far south as the temporary contractor's track allowed.

A similar arrangement would have existed at the south end, from the later Knowle Junction. The date of this connection is also unknown, but it is reasonable to assume the same dates stated above would have applied. (The wooden trestle 'viaduct' at Wickham, see No. 124, was no doubt provided as a means to transport material as far north as possible.)

The actual transfer arrangements from the LSWR are not reported. Presumably goods were delivered to the nearest railhead, Alton and possibly Fareham or Botley, and then 'tripped' to an interchange point where manhandling would have taken place. We also know the LSWR allowed their own goods wagons to travel over what was the temporary contractor's track - see images Nos. 102 /104.

Geographically however, the main sites of work were between West Meon and Privett. West Meon was also the physical half way point of the new railway and consequently considerable effort would have been needed to bring materials to this area. The only means this could be done was by road. The road distance to West Meon was approximately equal from the nearest railways at Bishops Waltham, Alton, and Petersfield, and it may have been the simple option as to the cheapest cost of transportation, the shortest time, greatest need, or the physical condition of the road and weight of goods relative to the gradients of the roads concerned that dictated the route chosen. (That south from Alton or north from Fareham were certainly the easiest.)

However, the roads of the late nineteenth century / early twentieth century were not metalled to the standard seen today - see No. 11 (this metalling took place from about 1920 onwards), consequently broken or crushed stone was the principal surface. The loads required to be carried would have been both numerous and heavy, meaning the condition of the road itself dictating some of these might only have been possible to be moved during dry periods.

8. Opposite top - An early Fowler steam traction engine of circa 1880. The view is posed outside the 'Sun Inn': likely to have been the hostility of that name on Filmore Hill, Privett. (See map No. 65.) Notice the front wheel of the trailer has been chocked. The load is a water tank. Water supplies would be destined to be a problem for the contractor especially on the northern half of the line. (See note with photo No. 46.) Former Privett resident, Alf Ayling, recalled the traction engines were preceded by a man with a red flag.

9. Opposite bottom - An Aveling-Porter 7 hp traction engine seen after arrival at

one of the contractors depots. The load is one of wagons that will be used to move materials, 'muck', during construction. ('Muck' was the term used by the navvies to describe any form of earth, soil, loam or rock etc that required to be shifted.) The fact a large pile of bricks is also stacked alongside is the reason for the conclusion this was a storage site for the contractor. The general appearance is not that of a railway yard from which goods would be collected. The source of the bricks used during the construction of the railway is not totally certain, it being likely that more than one supplier was used. Certainly it would have made sense for bricks to be secured locally and we know that Blanchard's from Bishops Waltham, together with a Mr. Church from Durley, supplied some of the bricks used. (Whether these were hauled by engine over the hilly route to Corhampton and then to site is not certain, possibly the longer route by rail to Botley and thence either to Fareham, Knowle or even Alton was considered preferable. At the time there were also several other brickworks local to the new railway, notably at Funtley and Bursledon.) Some of the surviving blue engineering bricks bear the stamping 'Bakemore', this may well have been a trademark used for this type of very hard brick brought in from elsewhere and intended for a specific use. Worth mentioning is that the actual contractor's railway engines, if needed for use before a physical connection with the rest of the system was available, would have been pulled by traction engine along the roadway, sometimes on low trailers, to the site of work, the engines having arrived on their own wheels at the nearest convenient station. Photographs of any such movements are unfortunately missing although, as there are views of the use of steam engines in the construction around the Privett and West Meon area, we can be certain this activity did occur. It is not known if Messrs Relf had a similar fleet of road steam engines used in the work or if locally owned road engines were used.

10. This page - Moving an accommodation hut, possibly even a type of navvy hut. Horses would have been used in addition to steam engines, the former taking the lighter loads and also being able to traverse softer ground. The location is not given.

11. Left - *The new bridge over the Alton - Fareham road at Farringdon, nowadays the A32. It is believed this is looking south. Officially this was Bridge No. 9 over what was known as the Gosport Road, having a brick arch and abutments. The width was 30' but it was built on a skew giving a total width of 43'. The maximum height was 18' 8". Of note are the metal railings, at the end of which is a section of wooden fence. The road surface is as per the comments on the previous page and would have caused some difficulty of passage during periods of inclement weather. Former Privett resident Alf Ayling, recounted that little traffic used the roads at the turn of the 20th century: what there was restricted to the occasional brewer's dray or miller's cart. What was in the 19th century referred to as the Coach Road from Alton, at the time took a route through several of the villages, including via Filmore Hill, Privett: see image No. 8, compared with the modern day. A contemporary report stated that further south at the village of Warnford, the road crossed the River Meon by means of a ford.*

12. Bottom left *and* **inset** *- Although published previously elsewhere, it is appropriate that this view of what would later be Butts Junction should be seen again and now in its proper context. The steam engine is an 0-6-0ST built by Messrs. Manning, Wardle Company Ltd. of Leeds and was one of three similar engines used by the contractor. (Details of these and the other steam engines used in the building of the line are given later in this book.) In the distance (insert below) is what appears to be another contractor's locomotive, probably a 0-4-0ST by the same builder, possibly the same engine as on the front cover. To the left is the new line towards Faringdon, straight ahead in the Mid Hants route to Medstead, Alresford and Winchester, and right that to Basingstoke.*

13. Believed to be the bridge No. 11 between Farringdon and East Tisted, carrying the new railway over the road from the present day A32 eastwards to Newton Valence. Aside from its railway identification number, this was known as the Horse and Groom Bridge, 53 miles, 34 chains from Waterloo. Constructed in the form of a brick arch and abutments and with a span of 20' but with a slight skew width thus making 21' 9". The maximum height was 19' 6". Together with the accompanying view of the Gosport Road bridge, this is one of the very few images of the line within the collection that are certain to be north of Privett. We know construction work had commenced in 1898 between the Butts outside Alton and Farringdon, the first major earthworks being the deep cutting south of East Tisted, the image seen on this page with its accompanying embankment not considered by the contractor to be a major earthwork. From 'THE STORY OF ALTON' by C W Hawkins, there is mention that construction of the Meon Valley line, "...brought many workmen to the town. Lodgings were difficult to obtain, and so a wooden hut was built in Rack Close (near to the area known as The Butts), to provide accommodation. The public houses did a roaring trade.....the local clergy made every effort to supply the spiritual needs of these men. In Alton, Miss Isabelle Lewis of Queens Road, held a regular Bible class at the lodging house, nicknamed 'The Navvies Hut', and she became very popular with the workmen." The name 'The Navvies Hut' would linger on with this wooden structure for many years. Nearby at Alton, there was also a sawmill, although it is not known if this supplied timber for the contractor.

14. Opposite page - *A navvy hut at the Hedge Corner crossroads south of Tisted where the roads from Monkwood and Steep cross the Gosport Road (the present day A32). Today there are lay-bys on the north west and south east sides of the crossroads, indicative of the time a skew arch carried the railway across the road and so necessitating a double bend at this point: the lay-bys being the remains of the main road at that time. Before the railway (and of course since the bridge has been demolished) it was and has since, become again a simple crossroads. Much debate has taken place as to the location of this view, the only other possible alternative being the crossroads at the West Meon Hut. But, and as is recounted later - see notes accompanying image No. 80, the West Meon Hut had existed with that name BEFORE the railway, whilst additionally there would seem to be no logical reason for the navvy camps not to be built as close to the site of work as possible - see image of Privett, Nos. 71 & 72. Consequently we can be certain of the location stated above. The fact that this would appear to be a single large building may mean it was erected for single men rather than a family.*

15. This page, top left - *The children of a navvy family from the Meon Valley line. It is a matter of regret that no names were recorded. The large family was by no means untypical, whilst a major concern of the various welfare workers was that of promiscuity. Despite the subject of sex being generally taboo for much of the Victorian era, the moral behaviour of some amongst the navvy fraternity was far from what was considered ideal.*

16. This page, top right - *Another, presumably family group, outside a navvy hut. Here the group certainly appear far better dressed, the children also having toys. In the background the men seen may well be lodgers.*

17. This page, right - *'On tramp' as it was called. A navvy family moving with their possessions from one site of work to the next. This is not necessarily Meon Valley but is contained within the David Foster-Smith collection. Men would learn of navvy work and arrive hoping to be selected. If successful, the contractor would provide rudimentary accommodation.*

18. Top left - *Another navvy hut / family, the image displaying some similarity to that of No.16. The close proximity to the actual site of work is apparent.*

19. Bottom left - *Possibly slightly out of geographic sequence, but of interest from several aspects. The view was contained in the album around the images that have been identified as being of West Meon and certainly before Misling-ford / Wickham. It would appear a double track formation has been provided on an embankment but it cannot be totally clear where this might be. (The impression is nearer to West Meon, possibly around the site of the viaduct, but as mentioned, the images in the album do not always appear to follow either a geographical or chronological sequence.) Whilst the Meon Valley route was generously laid out so far as gentle gradients and curves were concerned, only a single line of rails was provided. The bridges and tunnels were, however, made to double track width although many of the associated earthworks, cuttings especially, but also some of the embankments, were only sufficient for a single line for rails. The anticipated increase in traffic necessitating a second line of rails never materialised. But, and as mentioned, there were places where the availability of excavated spoil meant there was sufficient for a double track embankment to be provided. In consequence, could this be the approach to the West Meon Viaduct? Whatever, the existing rails are certainly only temporary: that on the right far closer to the edge of the embankment than would be acceptable for the finished track. A later single track, centrally placed on the embankment, would certainly appear feasible. In the background tipping is taking place, with a horse having moved at the wrong moment - hence the blur at the front of the wagon. On the right the curvature of the track may mean the rails here fell away sharply to allow wagons of muck to be lowered further down the slope: perhaps to consolidate the base. The main interest though is of course the photographer, caught by the actions of another carrying out similar actions. We cannot be certain who he might have been, although clearly more than one photographer was involved in recording the contemporary scene.*

20. Opposite page - *The Navvy Mission Hut at Privett. The actual location of this is not certain, although there is some evidence it may have been located in Sages Lane. The use of the building might, at first glance, be that of a place of worship, and whilst there can be little doubt that David Smith in his capacity as a lay-preacher would have indeed have led prayers, it must be recalled he was not an ordained Minister. In consequence it is likely he maintained close relations with the various local vicars - possibly even the latter coming to hold formal services in the mission hut rather risk the spectacle of the itinerant navvy appearing at the local church. The social position of the navvy had been decided upon decades earlier. But David Smith and his contemporary missioners had other uses for their mission huts. Here was the centre of the social life of the navvy, the intention being to keep the adult navvy, the 'nippers', and the navvy families occupied. Hence we know social events, gatherings, entertainment and lectures were commonplace. One contemporary report recording as follows, "Great rejoicing took place at the Navvy*

Mission on Boxing Day. The children assembled in the afternoon, and sat down to a splendid tea, which was admirably served by the workers and friends of the Mission. After the tea, the parents of the children and about sixty navvy friends came in to amuse them, and witness the stripping of the Christmas tree. Almost everybody was the recipient of a warm and useful garment, and every child also received some useful toy. These were purchased by the voluntary contributions of their parents, which amounted to £1. 16s. 9d., and a generous gift of a handsomely dressed doll to every girl by Miss G. Nicholson of Basing Park. The garments were kindly sent by Mrs. Longman of Clifton, Mrs. Troller of Kettering, Miss Stewart of Limpsfield, and Bliss Nisbett of Wimbledon. The tree was kindly given by Mr. W. Nicholson. Mr. W. Turner of Privett gave a splendid lot of cakes, and Mr. Farley provided an ample supply of oranges and nuts. During the evening, Mr. D. Smith (the Missionary), made an interesting speech. Speaking of the attendance at Sunday School, the children had put in about 70 per cent, and that they considered was very good considering the distance the children had to come. He was extremely grateful to all the friends and workers who had contributed to make the occasion such a delightful one. He then asked all present to show their appreciation by giving three hearty cheers. These were given in a right loyal way. The children dispersed about 8 o'clock, each receiving an orange and bun as they left the room."

21. *Navvy accommodation huts and works wagon at what is believed to be Privett. From the contemporary report reproduced reference image No. 20, it might have appeared that good relations existed between the landowners, railway company, contractor, missionary, and navvies, but behind the scenes we know this was far from the case. The name of Squire William Nicholson is mentioned, an influential landowner from nearby Basing Park (it was Nicholson who had succeeded in getting the name of the station here changed from its originally intended West Tisted to Privett before the line opened. No doubt the risk of non-cooperation over the sale of land won the day). Locally, he was also responsible*

for the truly magnificent Holy Trinity Church [inset] serving the village of Privett, complete with its 160' spire: the latter sometimes unkindly referred to as 'The Devil's Finger'. It was said that the impetus for its building came from the Nicholson family, whose fortune was amassed through their distillery business - perhaps a means of attempting to redress the balance of the 'evils of drink'! (The actual church is no longer in regular use as a place of worship but it is open for inspection). Whatever, the arrival of the contractor and with it a shortage of navvy labour was sufficient to tempt away many local farm labourers. According to Alan Earwaker in 'WEST MEON, SOME CHAPTERS IN ITS HISTORY', "...Suddenly the farm labourers found there was competition for their services. The contractors offered higher wages than the farmers and the latter, faced with the prospect of having to pay their men a living wage to keep them, resorted to threats and intimidation……..the landlords and farmers got together and agreed that if any of their men, or their families, went to work on the line, they would be thrown out of their cottages."[1] Later in the same work the author continues, "The late Mr William Martin told me his first job after leaving school was as a stoker on the construction engines that ran up and down the line, but he had to leave his home on the Basing Park Estate and lodge with an aunt in West Meon or his father would have been out on the street."

22. Opposite page, bottom right - The precursor of today's 'Home Delivery Service', supplies of food and other domestic requirements from local traders.

23. Top left and **24. Top right** - Navvies, the man on the left possibly a Foreman ('Ganger' was the term then in use), outside their huts / lodgings. The man with the lamp on the right may well have been a tunnel worker. Again, the close proximity of the accommodation huts to the railway will be noted. In some respects this was obvious as these buildings would invariably have to be placed on land purchased for the work.

1 - Notwithstanding a farm labourer of the period being considered fit due to amount of manual about involved in agriculture, it took a year for such a man to develop the strength equal the physical capabilities of a railway navvy.

25. *Left* and **26. *Right*** - *Construction at unreported locations. The fact that horses are being used would tend to imply this was an early stage of work - or an early stage at that specific location and prior to the work being sufficiently advanced to adjoin where locomotive access was possible. Apart from railway locomotives, at least one 'steam navvy' was used in the construction - see later images. This type of work, using horses, had changed little over the decades, indeed its very origins were with the canal 'navigators'. Referring to the specific images, the decorative bridles of the horses will be noted. The animals would also appear to be well kept - there must have been stables, a farrier and fodder store - presumably at each of the various depots along the construction site. The rails are lightly laid, literally placed on the excavated ground, but even so would allow the horse to pull what is a considerable load. The actual wagons - for which again a maintenance facility would have been required, could well be similar to the type seen being hauled by the traction engine earlier, (No. 9). All this 'muck' would have been shifted by hand, the previous comment about how long it took to turn a farm labourer into a navvy understandable. Reverting to the wagons again, these are of the tipping type, their contents pulled away to be deposited at the required spot, for this purpose temporary railway track would be laid, indeed a temporary connection can be seen leading to the face of the exaction on the left. The younger navvies were known as 'nippers'* [1], sometimes family members, other times local boys or even boys who had ventured from further afield. These individuals were rightly considered vulnerable and open to influence from some of the older men, hence David Smith formed a local 'Nippers League' [2] to try to keep them occupied outside working hours. The nippers did not have the same tasks as the men and would be employed on lesser duties, coupling wagons, placing and removing sprags, tipping wagons etc. It was reported that on 25 July 1901 at East Tisted, a 15 year old nipper by the name of Arthur William Hankin, was killed after being crushed between two ballast wagons. The nipper on the right is seen in somewhat precarious pose!*

1 - A 'nipper' was a general word meaning any young boy. The term was being used in naval language by at least 1800 to describe a boy seaman. By around 1820 it passed into general use to refer to any small boy and remained in use in this was in popular English until the 1950s.

2 - The term 'Nippers League' had been used elsewhere for the same purpose for many years.

27. One of what were probably several site workshops established by the contractor. Timber was an important requirement for railway work, not, as might be first considered, just for railway sleepers - such items were usually supplied by the railway company themselves using their standard fittings when the final permanent way was laid, but during the construction phase for the various temporary buildings as well as for shoring, essential in bridge and tunnel construction. Wherever possible wood this would be sourced locally, the men chopping down trees that were in their path which were, if suitable, used according to whether they were hard

or softwood type. In the view seen, the location is unreported, a set of wheels, the origins of which are not certain, is under repair at what is probably a blacksmith's forge. (The wheelset appears to be being held by the man directly on to a crankpin - yet the assembly appears too flimsy for even the smallest steam locomotive, especially considering the spilt spokes.)

28. Top right - *Navvies and their charges at what is clearly an established local stable. According to Dick Sullivan, navvies with specific skills, including that of leading and tending horses, were paid a premium wage.*

29. Bottom right - *Two horses at one of the contractor's depots. Notice the children in the background. The man on the extreme right has an oil (paraffin) hand lamp of a style that was used by the railways themselves right through to the 1960s. The dog at the feet of the man on the left is one of several dogs seen in various of the images from the collection. Pets perhaps, but no doubt also used for ratting and perhaps taking / hunting the occasional item of game. In an undated, but contemporary copy of the 'CHURCH TIMES', Peter Lombard or Canon Benham then well known as a native of West Meon, wrote as follows; "One goes on enlarging one's experience. Much as I have travelled in the course of my life, I never till this week saw a railway in the course of making. A charming scene of hill and dale, cornfield and wood, once as familiar to me as Cheapside is now, where I have rambled as a boy, picking nuts or birds-nesting, is today having a new line of the South Western Railway making right through it. Much of the beauty must of necessity be destroyed, but it would be idle to complain of that. I trust that the people will have reason to rejoice in the benefit. And the great chalk embankments, now as ugly as they can be, will soften-down and be clothed in green, and probably planted with trees. And I shall be able, if living, to run down in an hour or two to my native village, instead of having to go twelve miles over a rather rough road, as I used to do of yore, to the nearest railway station. I started from that village some years ago, at half-past seven one winter's morning, and was duly deposited in a third-class carriage at Winchester, which then rumbled along, stopping at every station, and I got to London but a very short time before evening set in.*

"It is curious and interesting to see the works going on. There are cuttings through the rising ground, and a vast amount of chalk is brought forth to level up the valley beyond. It looks all simple enough when you contemplate a finished line, and see the trains gliding so swiftly and easily over it, but see it in course of contraction, and what a prodigious work it is. I stood and watched the big carts coming out of the cuttings and along the chalk road already constructed; by some ingenious construction, which I might have understood had I climbed up sixty feet, these carts at a given point wheeled round, shot their load out on to the heap,

and went back for more. The heap looked no bigger for the addition. I wonder how many cart loads it takes to bridge that little valley over?

"But yet more interesting by far are the 'living agents.' The 'navvies' swarm in the streets of the quiet village, and it is a pleasure to have to write that the people like them and their ways, so far as I gathered. What is a navvy? The name, I find, originated with the Bridgewater canals. When these were made all over England to increase the water traffic the diggers were called 'navigators', because they were increasing the navigation, and the name has since got fixed upon the kindred occupation of railway-making. Perhaps it was because their clothes were of rough fustian, and their boots muddy, and their limbs stalwart, that the opinion got spread abroad that they were one and all brutalised fighters. Good Miss Marsh - whose name I have just been looking for in vain in the Directory of National Biography - taught the British people what fine fellows some of these navvys can be. And she has thereby gained a most honoured name in literature. There they were, as decent fellows as need be, so far as I saw; huts are scattered about all over the landscape, like the coops in a pheasant preserve, and here they will sojourn, till the road is finished.

"When they came swarming into the place, Dibbs, the general dealer, thought it a time to put up his prices at once, but it didn't answer, for Goahead and Brisk, two enterprising fellows, took a big house and converted it into a store as well as restaurant, and they are hard at work with their spec. The squire took me over the place, and it was very interesting. First we went into a quondam stable, now converted into a bake house. There is an enormous machine, capable (so the attendant told us) of baking 3,000 2lb. loaves a day. Then we went into another room wherein were hanging a vast number of joints of meat. The general result is summed up that a good dinner of meat, vegetables and bread can be supplied for sixpence, and a pint of wholesome beer with it for twopence. A good many of them are total abstainers, and there was a perfect army of bottles of beverages to suit them. We went through the stores - stationery, clothing, groceries, even skipping ropes for children - I saw all these things as I walked through. There are carts which go a round of fifteen miles a day to the several centres of navvy labour to carry the bread and meat. Altogether a very pleasant visit, and I am looking forward in hope of another run down when the line shall be finished." [1]

1. No record of a second visit appearing in print has been found.

30. Above - *Possibly the same contractor's compound as seen on the previous page, but clearly also a timber stacking ground - notwithstanding the man with the axe, from the look of the trunks and the pile of planks in the background there was also a sawmill nearby, probably on site. 'Nippers' are also present although it is not clear what the boy in the centre is carrying. Behind the planks may be the top of a derrick indicating this could well be the site of one of the tunnel excavations. If so it would also explain the planks, to be used for tunnel shoring.*

32. Below - *This image appears in the David Smith album, again without caption or explanation. A sleeping or drunken navvy, possibly recorded for use in his lantern slide lectures to emphasize the effect and risk associated with alcohol consumption. We do not know if David Smith was himself teetotal.*

33. Right - *Break (snap) time with the men slaking their thirst from bottle and flagon. The man standing, and seemingly preaching, may be David Smith although there is some doubt as to the similarity. Whatever, this is one of several similar scenes showing either David Smith or another in like role, keeping the men occupied both during and outside work.*

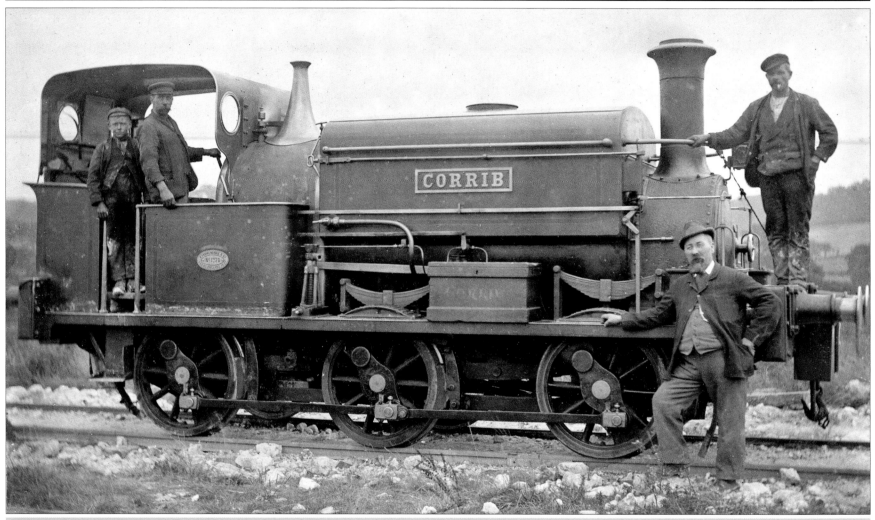

*Approximately eight steam locomotives were engaged by the contractor Relf for use in the construction, although not necessarily all at the same time. The Industrial Railway Society (IRS) in their publication 'HANDBOOK J - INDUSTRIAL LOCOMOTIVES OF CENTRAL SOUTHERN ENGLAND', affords a useful starting point for detail of these, supplemented, although sometimes also contradicted, by the works records of the specific locomotive manufacturers. **34. Above** and **35. Opposite** - 'Corrib' likely to have been named after the river in the west of Ireland, was a Manning Wardle (MW) 0-6-0ST to their 'K' type design, works No. 1220 of 24 July 1891. Originally supplied new to C. Braddock Contr. in Ireland, it was built to the Irish 5' 3" gauge but was re-gauged to the standard 4' 8½" by its next owner Messrs T H Falkiner Contr., later passing to H M Nowell & Co. Contr. The engine became the property of R T Relf at an unknown date, perhaps especially for the Meon Valley contract in 1898/9. It is thought to have subsequently been passed on to H Lovatt Contr., who was responsible for the construction of the Ludgershall - Tidworth line. David Smith may well have followed its passage as his photographic albums contain an image of an inspection train near Tidworth. Whilst at work on*

the Meon Valley the livery is not known, but may well have been a dark brown. Notwithstanding the inevitable splashes of chalk, the engine is in fine condition, with the right hand view displaying evidence of a rudimentary attempt at weather protection. It appears the same man, presumably the driver, is seen in the cab in the left hand view and on the ground in the right hand view. The two types of buffers will be noted, conventional and, within these, 'dumb' or solid buffers, the latter of a greater surface area. This was necessary on the lightly laid contractor's track when hauling or propelling contractors wagons of the type previously seen. A screw jack is also present on the running plate of the left view for use when necessary. (Derailments were probably commonplace on the light temporary track). Maintenance would have been carried out by the driver as well as other contractor's staff, whilst as the work was ongoing, it is very unlikely a specific locomotive depot was established. Unless moved by road, or transferred around by the LSWR, some of the engines may well have been delivered and consequently used solely around specific locations on the contract, as it would not have been until late in the actual work that the whole could have been considered a through route.

36. Left - *This time it is an Manning Wardle built 0-4-0ST of their 'F' type that is seen. Smaller and consequently lighter than the 'K' type, it was one of three MW engines delivered new, reported as 'To R T Relf Contr. Fareham'. (These engines were two 'F' type and one 'K' type.) Whilst at first glance it may appear that this confirms their use on the southern end of the MV construction, and indeed there is photographic evidence later of a member of the 'F' type close to the temporary wooden trestle at Wickham (see No. 124), it must be recalled Messrs R T Relf were also responsible for building the Fareham deviation line at the same time as the MV route. Possibly locomotives were exchanged between the two sites, or may even have been restricted to one or another.*

37. Bottom - *Another engine of similar type, 'Annie'. (Names, often related to the location of the work, were carried over from a previous owner, or in the case of a person, carried some significance to the owner / previous owner). The fact this engine bears a plate indicated 'Renewed' in 1899, must indicate it had been built some time before that. The most likely candidate being MW Works No. 1343 of 1897. If so, this engine came from Messrs. Pauling & Co. having worked on the Stert - Westbury contract and after being employed in Hampshire, subsequently returned westwards to Messrs. C J Wills & Sons building the Castle Cary - Langport line.*

38. Right - *Seen from the rear is what is possibly a MW 0-6-0ST but this time with an open cab - and lining on the buffer beam! The position of the fire irons will be noted. Of equal interest is the location, certainly the approach to one of the tunnels, possibly that at West Meon. On close inspection at least six navvies can be seen in various positions on the cutting side - excluding the man on the skyline and the one on the right: the latter clearly identified from his clothes as certainly not a navvy. With a rough passageway cut through the chalk, the men are engaged in facing the cutting sides, 'muck' being dropped either directly into wagons in front of the engine or on to the ground where it will be shovelled by other men into the wagons. See also note re buffers at No. 104.*

39. Bottom - *Peckett & Sons No. 505 'Blanche', an 0-4-0ST of February 1893 to their 'M4' class. This engine was supplied new to W S Jenkin of Bodmin, and passed to Relf at an unreported date. Its subsequent disposal is also unknown. Messrs Relf were active on several railway contracts in the south west and consequently it may have been acquired through one of these.*

40. Opposite page and **41. Top left -** In No. 40 we see 'Blanche' outside the contractor's yard. From the group present it would appear this may have been an inspection party - the state of the clothing and footwear of the lady present might indicate after the return. None of the persons seen can be identified by name - could the lady perhaps even be Miss Nicholson?, but in appearance at least three have been depicted in earlier views. (See Nos. 23, 23 and 39.) No. 41 shows the engine carrying a group of observers on a tour of the work, probably a different group to that seen in the main view. From No 42. we know this same engine was working in the area of the tunnels, thus the lamps seen being carried by some of the men could well have been to allow the visitors to peer into the tunnel excavation.

42. Top right - 'Blanche' almost dwarfed by the depth of cutting and approaching the face of what is believed to be the north end of Privett Tunnel. (See also comments captions 62 and 63.)

43. Bottom right - The same engine at an unreported location. The storm sheet to the side of the cab will be noted, as will the re-railing jack and wagon sprags loose on the front framing. Notice also the holes for the bolts that would hold conventional buffers: replaced here with what are massive timbers blocks. All the engines in this series of images, when seen from the front, have a large oil lamp in place.

44. *'Jubilee', another MW 0-4-ST, works number 991 of 1887 and believed to have been the oldest locomotive used on the construction. This engine was supplied new to J Wooley of Wrexham and passed through several hands before ending up with Relf. The name is thought to have been carried from the outset and is synonymous with the year of its build. Some reports imply only one man was employed as driver / fireman, the second man present, seen both here and on the opposite page, a 'nipper', who would assist with coupling and spragging - witness said item seen being carried. (More likely the 'nipper' was a general assistant to the driver, acting as stoker [fireman] when necessary. The limited coal capacity of the contractors engines meant coal would have been needed to be available at the contractors depots.) Braking was by hand only and activated on just the rear wheels. Due to the rough condition of the track and weights involved, allied to the limit brake power available, speeds would have been slow.*

45. *The same view as seen on the cover, but now dealt with so far as the locomotive is concerned. This would appear to be another MW 0-4-0ST but this time totally cab-less and instead fitted with a wooden storm guard. (Different levels of finished specification could be requested at the time the order was placed). According to the records in the IRS book previously referred to, four MW 0-4-0ST locomotives were thought to have been used. No. 11, 'Jubilee': works No. 2343 has already been illustrated and accounted for, so this may be the fourth, No. 10. If so, it is works No. 1419 of 1897, delivered new to R T Relf at Fareham. Whilst it has been mentioned that Relf had the contract for the double track Fareham deviation line, the view above is still said to be MV construction, due to the strata of chalk compared with the clay encountered at Fareham. It has been mentioned that approximately eight locomotives were used on the contract, all to standard gauge. 'Blanche' seen on previous pages, does not appear in the IRS listings, however a 1900 0-6-0ST 'Evelyn' by Hudswell Clark does, and of which there are no illustrations.*

46. Children at the site of what was later to be Privett station, destined to be the highest point on the line, at 518 feet above sea level. The view is looking south: the spire of Privett church visible in the middle distance, and to the right, the curve of the cutting that will take the line towards Privett tunnel. Notice also the chalk excavation for the latter in the distance. The site is a veritable mix of scenes, the navvy huts on the right, water tank, a single contractor's wagon, and temporary track. The line disappearing behind the children may have been used to carry 'muck' to form the new road embankment leading to the Nicholson residence at Basing Park from the nearby crossroads - the latter were known as 'The Jumps'. Basing Park house was requisitioned during WW2 to accommodate WRNS personnel. Subsequent to this it was empty for some 20 years until demolished around 1965. The new road however, still survives. A 1909 Ordnance Survey plan of the immediate area indicates the presence of an old gravel pit around the area of the extreme left of the picture. It is not known if this was in use at the time of construction. A water supply to the construction site was taken from pipes laid from the village pond. With the route incomplete we can be certain this scene was recorded at least before 1901: see notes accompanying images 62 and 63.

47. *Top* and **48. *Right*** - *With no index or captions to the albums, it is difficult to be 100% certain as to the which of the two tunnels are seen under construction or, for that matter, which end! (Believed to be West Meon above and Privett right.) The readers indulgence is therefore craved. What we do know is that both tunnels were dug from both ends, whilst excavation of the longer 1,057yd Privett tunnel (differing reports vary the length by a yard or so either way), was assisted with a vertical shaft part way along its length. West Meon tunnel was shorter, at 539 yards. Various commentators on the MV railway have in the past, also slightly misled the reader by inferring that at the mid point of Privett Tunnel it was impossible to see light at either end due to the route making an 'S' shape within. This is not strictly true. Yes, there was a point mid way when daylight was lost, but this was due to a curve of 40 chains on entering, easing to 70 chains part way through. Trains thus entered the tunnel on a 1 in 100 falling gradient from the north and on a right hand curve, and continued on this same right hand curve, albeit with a change of radius, to the exit.*

49. Top left - At the time the MV route was proposed by the LSWR, Messrs. Wm. R Galbraith and E Andrews were engaged by the railway to produce an 'Estimate of Expense' for the work. This is reproduced in Ray Stone's book so need not be repeated here, although certain extracts may be appropriate. Firstly the contract (referring just to the main Butts Junction to Knowle Junction section), was estimated to involve the excavation of 1,213,120 cu.yds. of chalk and soft soil for cuttings. A similar figure, 1,261,500 cu.yds. of material was estimated to be required for embankments. Both these figures included roadways where appropriate. The land required was in the order of 270 acres, the cost put at £52,250. The total cost of the work, allowing also a 10% contingency, was put by the engineers as amounting to £400,000. The estimate is dated 29 December 1896 and thus predates the passing of the Parliamentary Act authorising construction. (The costs of the tunnels are referred to reference Nos. 62 and 63.) This view seen here is another puzzler. In the original albums, most of the MV images are contained in what we may conveniently refer to Book 1. The odd one also being duplicated in Books 2 and 3, whilst also in No. 2 is one image specifically quoted as being MV related but which does not appear elsewhere. This top view is the puzzle. It appears in Book 2 without comment and is unlike any other contract location recorded by David Smith. The conclusion then is that this could be excavation at the top of Privett tunnel perhaps even with the derrick seen on the opposite page, hidden by the mound.

50. Bottom far left and **51. Bottom near left** - Two more puzzlers. It is believed the right hand view is the approach to Privett tunnel with the surveyor and his assistant(s) paused in their labour for the photographer. The location of the left hand image is not certain, but it is interesting not least for the simple passing loop provided. As mentioned before, the track layout used by the contractors was simple and basic, with no ballast and intended to be simply functional. No doubt derailments were a commonplace and accepted occurrence: hence the re-railing jacks on the locomotives. But, what makes these two images unique amongst the collection is they show what appears to be narrow gauge track (one other image with the same track gauge appears at No. 67.) There is no record of narrow gauge steam engines having been used at any stage and the conclusion then is that this may have been a section where locomotive access was difficult or impractical to achieve until the tunnel(s) were complete. This may just have applied to the route from the south end of Privett tunnel and the Petersfield Road (A272) Bridge (See also Nos. 67, 74 & 75.) The cross beam serves as bracing against the cutting side.

52. Left, 53. Top Right, and **54. Bottom Right** - *In connection with the excavation of Privett Tunnel, a single vertical shaft was sunk, eventually reaching a depth of 90' and some 12' square. This was later filled in. All the excavated material for both tunnels was of relatively soft material and consequently no blasting was required, the disadvantage to this being that shoring was essential - see Nos 62 and 63. The location of this shaft was in a field to the rear of what was, post 1970, the Privett village shop.*

55. Left and **56. Right** - *The shaft leading down into the working. Some scale of the size can be gained from the man conveniently standing against the edge. Men, materials and muck were lifted up and down by bucket and as is seen on the opposite page, horses were also at work in the headings. The size of the opening was no doubt determined by the need to lower wagons into the workings. Perhaps slightly surprisingly the option of leaving the space open as ventilation was not later acted upon, although this would have involved lining the chamber with bricks or similar. Another reason this was not done may have been pressure from Squire Nicholson. (Despite seemingly negative comments about Nicholson earlier, it should be mentioned that as he expanded his ownership of land and farms in the area he re-equipped these with new and well thought out buildings together with proper drainage and a pump in the scullery from which safe water could be obtained.)*

Top: Left to right - Nos. 57 to 59.
Bottom: Left to right - Nos. 60 & 61.
Views around the top of the shaft. Reports accompanying the death of Navvy George Brown, see next page, refer to the vertical shaft as being "...the central one of three being bored ...". It is likely this was meant to refer to the one vertical shaft and the two horizontal headings then being driven, one from each end. The location of the vertical shaft seen, was referred to at the time as being in Little Collins Field. (To subscribe to the idea that there were three vertical shafts for a tunnel just over 1,000 yards long would indicate one and possibly two shafts would then be expected to have been sunk for West Meon tunnel of half the length. This would seem most unlikely.) A steam crane / derrick is seen in use.

62. Top and **63 Bottom** - Two remarkable views recorded inside one, or perhaps even, both, tunnels. In the lower view David Smith is clearly identified, again affording council to the men. Lighting and exposure for these images over a century ago would have been interesting, presumably the burning of a magnesium flash was the only option. Under normal circumstances the men would work by candles. In the top view, the massive shoring necessary is seen, the men mostly standing on unexcavated chalk. In the lower right hand corner of the same image is what is the top of the rectangular opening through which wagons might pass. It is unlikely the steam engines were able to work in the tunnel or indeed such practice would be desirable, consequently a line of wagons would have been pushed in by the engine and then hand-propelled as necessary. The situation would have changed as the bore was complete and lined. On the lower left hand side of the same view can be seen the chalk strata. The curve of the roof gives some indication as to the size of the void in which the men worked. The lower view shows a standard gauge track and rudimentary vice and workbench, some of the men sitting on what are saw benches. At the time the December 1896 estimate was prepared , the two tunnels were estimated to account for £39,900, or 10% of the cost of the whole route. When complete, both were fully lined and although, because the external portals are seen to be of brick, the temptation is to believe this material was used throughout, within, sections of both tunnels were lined in concrete. This comment over the use of concrete is of specific relevance for later. Again from the report of the death of Navvy Brown, is the information that in January 1899 work was taking place to sink the shaft previously referred to. It is very likely that with the tunnels seen as the principal engineering work on the route, work would likely have commenced on these at the outset and so confirming the earlier belief that there were several simultaneous sites of work. So far as actual progress is concerned, at the north end of the tunnel at least, a contemporary report reproduced in Ray Stone's book and quoting 1900 but unfortunately not the month or day, refers to an undated incident when labourer Arthur Sunidge, aged 23, died from injuries received in Privett tunnel as he and John Franklin were collecting trucks with an engine. Both men were riding on a wagon furthermost from the propelling engine. They bumped into an empty truck and Sunidge fell between the wagons and was run over. He died from his injuries. This would mean that image No. 42 would have been taken around 1900, and as the same engine is seen in Nos. 40 and 41, the inspection tour was probably of the line north of Privett with the depicted contractor's depot also confirmed as dealing with the northern half of the route. It is in consequence of a further accident that we know the route, when complete from Privett at least as far back as Farringdon, was to convey on a light engine, an injured navvy who had been run over at Privett. The un-named man, whose legs had both been severed below the knees, was reported as having been smoking his pipe throughout the journey on the engine and at Farringdon was transferred to a horse and wagon for the journey to the hospital at Alton. Unfortunately be was found to be dead on arrival. Finally, and again on an unreported date, two navvies were seriously hurt in the deep cutting north of Privett tunnel. Richard Allen, aged 25, was trimming trucks when caught in the chest by another truck. He too was put on an engine and conveyed to Farringdon, but died on the way to Alton .

64. *The image of George Brown, aged 29, who was killed in the sinking of the vertical shaft for Privett tunnel. The accident was reported in a number of newspapers, as far afield as the 'Belfast Newsletter', 'Western Mail', and 'Northern Echo'. The latter, of 23 January 1899, referred to two men being buried, with the names given and, "...although large gangs are at work it is feared the bodies will not be reached for several days." On the following day, the same newspaper reported that one of the men, James Owen, had been released alive. The 'HAMPSHIRE TELEGRAPH & SUSSEX CHRONICLE' for 28 January 1899, which newspaper report has not previously been commented upon before, affords full detail of the accident as well as much useful information as to the working conditions prevailing at the time. "MEON RAILWAY DISASTER - A FATAL FALL OF EARTH - WORKMANS MARVELOUS ESCAPE. At a late hour on Friday night an accident occurred on the new Meon Valley Railway at Privett, a fall of earth entombing two men, named James Owen, and Brown. Owen, is a married man with two children, and Brown was an Army Reserve man, and the two were working for Messrs. Relf and Son, contractors. They were engaged in a shaft for a tunnel, forty feet deep and twelve feet square, when, without any warning, the sides fell in and buried them. The tunnel is to be 1,056 yards long, and the central shaft, in which Owen and Brown were working, lies immediately behind the church at Privett, (clearly this last statement is incorrect as seen from the accompanying map). and only a short distance from the residence of Mr. W Nicholson, M.P., at Basing Park. It being a very rough night, only four men turned up at their work, and while Owen and Brown descended the shaft, the other two remained at the top, one being the banksman, who looks after the working of the crane and the other the engine driver. The unfortunate men in the shaft had only been at, the bottom a short time, when the banksman heard cries from below, and to his horror discovered that the sides of the shaft had collapsed, burying Owen and Brown, He immediately cried out for assistance, and Constable Gray, of the Hants Constabulary, went to the spot. It was apparent that immediate relief was impossible, owing to the amount of earth which had fallen in, the quantity being estimated at 30 tons. Mr. Stevens, the foreman, lives in one of the specially erected huts near at hand and he soon started the night-gangs of the other shafts at work on the one which had fallen in, the rescue party being hard at work at a very early hour on Saturday morning. The men were working in four hour shifts, but owing to the size of the shaft it was not possible to put many at work at one time and several days were expected to elapse before the men were reached. Owen was rescued alive on Monday. He was brought to the surface at six o'clock in the morning, having worked his way up towards his rescuers. He was unhurt, but stated that his fellow workman, Brown, died on Saturday. THE SURVIVOR'S THRILLING STORY. Owen experienced a miraculous escape from death, but he appeared little the worse for his imprisonment of sixty hours and on reaching the surface was able to walk to his home, a distance of three miles. He states that when the staging in the pit showed signs of giving way, his mate Brown and he got into their bucket at the bottom of the shaft and shouted to the banksman to haul them up. The weather was very boisterous and he concludes that owing to the high wind their cries were not heard at first by the man at the top of the shaft. Presently the earth began to fall in, carrying away the struts and imprisoning both men at the bottom of the deep pit. The struts fell clear of Owen, who remained unhurt under the pile of timber, but unfortunately Brown was jammed fast by the legs, a circumstance which rendered his escape impossible. When the rescuers reached Owen*

65. Bottom right - *Taken from the Tithe map of Privett, dated 1840. This is included as it indicates many of the locations referred to in the text, including The Sun Inn (indicated). The incorrect attribution of the tunnel shaft as being located behind the church at Privett can also be seen (indicated). The western boundaries of the parish are shown by the thick black lines as in the route of the present day A32 and A272.*
(Map from 'Froxfield & Privett - A Taste of History'. John Day / Tony Newman.)

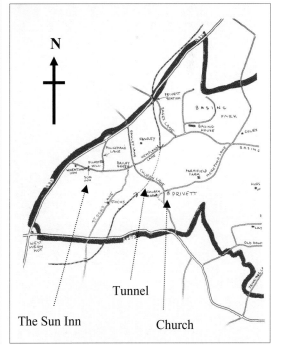

N

The Sun Inn

Tunnel

Church

he had made his way upwards with the aid of a pocket-knife only, cutting through about 25ft. of debris. In accomplishing this difficult, painful, and tedious task he cut four planks of wood right through the centre. Owen states that Brown spoke to him last on Saturday, when he wished him "good-bye," and said he was dying fast. He asked his comrade to convey a loving message to his sister. THE SURVIVOR AT THIS INQUEST. The County Coroner (Mr. Edgar Goble) held an inquest in the School Room at Privett on Thursday, investigating the death of George Brown, 29. The survivor gave a thrilling account of awful experience in the shaft from Friday night until Monday morning and described the manner in which he worked his way towards the top through tons of earth with the aid of a small penknife. The Jury returned a verdict of 'Accidental Death,' and exonerated everyone from blame." Other contemporary sources afford further detail including that "Mr Relfe (Jnr)......was early in attendance on Saturday". Following his release, Owen was reported as "dazed and exhausted but he had received no bodily injuries whatsoever. He was at once taken to the house of Mr. Isaac Stevens (Foreman) of Sages Lane, Privett where he ate a good breakfast. (Another reports comments Owen was so hungry following his release he ate six loaves of bread.) He afterwards went, with his wife and children, to his house (at East Tisted), walking nearly all the way." (The HAMPSHIRE ADVERTISER for 25/1/1899 carried the same story but in addition reported that "His wife (Owen's) and children, who had abandoned all hope, were overcome by news of his safety. The search parties are working with renewed hope to find the other entombed man.") The number of fatalities thus associated with Privett tunnel and its immediate area was four. (The total of other injuries is not known.) It appears all of this disturbed a number of the men and even caused some to leave, preferring safer work elsewhere, albeit for less money. (Tunnel men were paid a premium.) Not withstand the fact that at its peak some 600 men were engaged on the construction overall, it appears the contractor was concerned as to progress (was there a financial penalty involved for late completion of the contract and indeed did the LSWR have to seek powers for an extension of time relative to completion?). Whatever, according to Ray Stone again, the prospect of further tunnel work being required 'just around the corner' on the West Meon tunnel, meant that mechanical aids, in the form of steam excavators ('steam navvies') were apparently brought into use. If this comment is taken as literally correct, then it means the work up to this time and all the way south from Butts Junction had been excavated by hand. It also means the images showing steam navvies must therefore be post-1899. In some respects this would appear strange. A contractor would usually be expected to use the most labour-saving devices: an excavator would have achieved the work of numerous men. **67. Opposite page, top left -** We now get the one of the most interesting facets of the construction, the proof that a narrow gauge line was at one time used in connection with the construction from the south end of Privett tunnel. This is as is seen in photos 50 and 51 and also on the opposite page - top. None of the images seen in this book have been 'doctored' for scale in any way and consequently by comparing the width of the horse standing between the track it can be clearly seen the trackwork has to be less than the standard 4' 8½" gauge applicable to all the known steam locomotives on the construction. Instead this gauge would seem to be in the order of just 2'

66. Here the temporary way has been laid at the base of the cutting - the latter supported by cross timbers, the men standing on these and then knocking muck down into the waiting wagons below. Possibly the north end of Privett tunnel. If the location is correct then these wagons would later be removed by locomotive, but through what is of course a very narrow gap. Hence the explanation also why it was necessary for men to travel on the front wagon of a train bringing empties - they could then couple easily. A century plus later, it is tempting to make comparisons with the health and safety culture of today and this has been avoided for deliberate reasons. One comment may however be made - where indicated, could that be a man crouched and passing between the wagons and the cutting side?

- in itself a commonly used narrow gauge. The reason for this could well have been access problems for the excavations at the south end of Privett tunnel: almost the nearest road being the present day A272. It may also be assumed the narrow gauge was replaced by standard gauge prior to the permanent trackwork being laid. Compared with Privett tunnel, the building of West Meon tunnel proceeded quickly with just a few, non fatal, accidents to the men.

68. Right - Here the scene is from the south side of what will become the approach to West Meon viaduct - the south portal of West Meon tunnel visible in the distance. A small contractor's yard is also visible together with equipment and some wagons: under a glass these look to be of standard gauge. (See also No. 90.)

69. Left - *Again slightly out of context, but included to show a similar scene as No. 67, although this time looking south from Privett tunnel towards the A272. In some parts, the final slope of the cutting is complete, although men can also still be seen on its sides. The track here is certainly now standard gauge. The temporary double track passing loop disappearing into the distance gives a good impression of how a double track Meon Valley route might have appeared.* **70. Above -** *Purported to be inside Privett tunnel, but more accurately the approach, with supporting timbers across an early stage in making the cutting, again to standard gauge. Water supplies were a problem north of West Meon where no streams flowed on the dry chalk uplands. Consequently it was necessary to sink artesian wells 100' or more deep to tap water which was essential for the contractors locomotives and equipment. These wells were later used as the basis for the water supply to the stations and railway cottages.*

71. Above *and* **72. Right -** *Navvy huts perched precarious above the side of the excavations on the south side of West Meon tunnel, their position once having looked out over grassland. (Under a glass washing can be seen fluttering in the breeze on what was clearly a warm day.) At the entrance a horse can be seen having drawn a load of empty wagons ready for refilling. At least 18 men are also present in the right hand view with standard gauge track. (Presumably the wagons were spragged, the horse was unhitched, and the wagons pushed one at a time by human muscle power to their prescribed position within the workings. Horsepower again being used to draw them out again. When full, controlling loaded wagons on a steep 1 in 100 gradient, must have been required consumate skill.)*

73. Left - *Possibly the north end of West Meon tunnel* [1] *, but in which case before the bridge carrying Vinnells Lane was built. Whilst slightly out of sequence so far as the next major part of our story, that of the navvy camp at West Meon, it is convenient to include the last of the tunnel views first. From the shape of the spectacle plate, the locomotive could well be 'Jubilee', see No. 44, in which case also we now have evidence of its use south of Privett. Work on West Meon tunnel may not have commenced until most of the excavation for Privett had been completed. West Meon tunnel was built on an 80 chain curve throughout and a 1 in 100 gradient falling towards West Meon station. This undated newspaper cutting within the David Smith album records the completion, although from its slightly ambiguous title the impression, incorrectly, might have been gained that there was a junction of actual railways at WM. This was not the case. "JUNCTION OF WEST MEON TUNNEL' (actually meaning the joining of the tunnel excavations from each end) - A supper was held in the dining rooms of Lynch House (Lynch House lay on the south side of the road between the villages of West Meon and East Meon) on Tuesday in last week in celebration of the junction of the Westmeon tunnel. Mr. Edward Ismay, cashier, presided, and there were about 50 present. After supper the Royal toast was drunk, and then the health of the firm, Messrs. R. T. Relf and Son. Mr:*

Ismay next proposed the health of Mr. Avery, the engineer, and Mr. Drayton, the tunnel foreman, and, in the course of his remarks, congratulated them on their successful work, and said he had been on public works for twenty years and had never seen a better junction. A tunnel on an acute curve is always a very difficult piece of work, and Mr. Avery and Mr. Drayton had made a junction within half an inch! The health's of Mr. Avery and Mr. Drayton were drunk with musical honours, and both suitably responded. The supper, supplied by Messrs. Beaten and Smyth, went off splendidly, all the men enjoyed themselves, and there was plenty of singing. The evening closed with a vote of thanks to the chairman, proposed by Mr. Avery."

1. Another possible location could be emerging from the southern end of the cutting at East Tisted!

74. Opposite bottom and **75. This page** - *Tipping wagons of muck on an unreported embankment. In 74 the wagon has been run up on to a wooden stop, momentum causing the load to be discharged forward. In No. 75 it appears the load has been discharged but final clearing is taking place.*

76. Top left: 77 Top right: 78. Lower left:

79. Opposite - *Spoil tipping, the location(s) cannot be confirmed although it is tempting to say this was in the area of the A272 Petersfield Road Bridge. Ray Stone comments that commensurate with the amount of muck removed from Privett tunnel, the embankment soon reached the road, but progress was then slowed until the arch was complete. Possibly the engineers had decided on an arch and embankment instead of viaduct at this point simply as a means of using spoil. At the opposite end of Privett tunnel, so much had been excavated that cartloads of chalk were run to a site just north of the station, under the main road (A32) and to a point north of the later railway cottages. Here it was tipped between the road and railway forming what was known locally as 'spoil bank'. Further south at Meonstoke, close to overbridge No. 48 at a point where Frys Lane becomes New Road, a small mount of surplus muck can still be seen today on the east side of the route. No doubt similar mounds exist elsewhere, whilst north of Corhampton parts of the embankment may have been deliberately widened, either to use surplus spoil or perhaps even for reasons of stability. In No. 79 part of a simple turnout is seen. The man second from left in No. 76 has evident musical leanings. In No. 77, a wagon sprag is seen in use.*

THE WEST MEON NAVVY CAMP

The amount of spoil excavated from Privett tunnel was the reason for the well known embankment / bridge that still survives today across the A272, (Bridge No. 28) although the trackbed is nowadays topped with trees. This 'road tunnel' is 167' in length is in fact a brick arch with concrete abutments, the latter faced with brick. The line of rails 64' above road level with the arch giving 22' 2" clearance at road level.

Close to the railway on the north side of the modern A272 and immediately west of the new line was the site of a large navvy camp. This is described in WEST MEON, SOME CHAPTERS IN ITS HISTORY. "There was a camp of huts built for the navvies in the field north of the A272 next the railway, opposite the Cottage Loaf Café. (this was a wayside, transport type café, that existed for many years on the south side of the A272 just west of the A272 overbridge. It would certainly not have been present at the time the railway was built but was mentioned in the later description to allow some 'placement'. The café ceased trading around the 1970 period.) There were many drunken fights at the pubs, particularly at the Hut and the Horseshoes at Woodlands (near Privett), the two nearest to the camp. Between January 1900 and April 1901 there are five burials recorded in the Church register, with 'navvy huts' as the address, two of them babies under one year. (Buried at the western end at the top of West Meon Churchyard: 8-1-1900: William Baxter aged 45, 12-2-1900: Mark Westaway aged 66, 18-4-1900: Frederick Simons aged 3 months, 20-10-1900: William George Beech aged 9 months: 6-12-1900, Joseph Doughty aged 41. ….…..In the village the locals would not drink with the navvies. At the White Horse at the crossroads, a hut was built in the sunken garden next the road for the navvies and the locals went indoors. Most Saturday nights there was trouble. Sometimes the local police were able to stop it, sometimes they turned a blind eye." This type of behaviour is contrary to that reported at No. 73, where it appears a jolly evening was had by all, but possibly not including many of the actual navvy brethren. For many years there has been a public house approximately half a mile west of the A272 road crossing named the 'West Meon Hut' and which has understandably given rise to the belief this was where the navvy camp was situated, also where the pub had taken its name from. This assertion is incorrect. A report in the HAMPSHIRE TELEGRAPH & SUSSEX CHRONICLE for 31 July 1896, some time before the railway had even been authorised, has the following entry, "The Hambledon Hounds will meet on Monday at Highden Cross Roads: Wednesday, Shedfield Common, Friday, Horndean: Saturday, Westmeon hut; at 11.30 each day.[1]" The term 'Hut' possibly one of much earlier origin and meaning a place of refreshment or a restocking facility for drovers. **80. Above: 81 to 84. Opposite**. Believed to be the navvy camp in the vicinity of the A272 / site of construction at West Meon. The presence of the tents is not explained - single men, temporary accommodation before the erection of wooden huts etc? **Inset on this page** - the completed bridge over the Petersfield Road (A272) between the Privett and West Meon tunnels clearly showing the height of embankment above the bridge itself. The view is taken from the 1903 RAILWAY MAGAZINE, which featured an article on the new line, then only just opened. What is interesting in the chalk has already been toned down with by the addition of topsoil to encourage growth.

1. Some records refer to the West Meon Hut being known as The George Inn at some stage, although the archives may also be confusing the name with what is now the 'George & Falcon' and was indeed previously 'The George' at nearby Warnford.

Top to bottom, left to right, Nos. 85 to 88.
No. 85 and 87 two more views of the tented encampment: conditions would not have been ideal other than during good weather. We are also told the work was delayed on occasions due to periods of inclement weather which caused slipping of the cuttings and embankments. The Navvy mission hut is another puzzle. Possibly at West Meon, we know such a facility did exist at West Meon as it was reported as having been opened on 11 August 1900.

The lower right view was taken on the opening day - at West Meon Mission hut perhaps?. Another comment however, is that the building shown above was located at Farringdon. If so this would make a total of three mission halls on the one line. The man on the cycle outside the hut does not appear to totally resemble David Smith, but as has been stated, others of like persuasion may well have been active, David Smith's 'parish' perhaps concentrated in the area of Privett - but that does not then explain why his albums contain views outside the area!

89. *A Church Army wagon outside New Inn meadow at West Meon - now the car park of the Thomas Lord. Was this a travelling mission, or as referred previously, did different religious groups hold sway at different locations? The significance of the name of the caravan 'WINCHESTER II' is also unknown, although possible as simple of the second wagon of the Winchester Company.*

90. Left (Inset above) - We now get to one of the most interesting finds from this remarkable collection, the story of the viaduct at West Meon, the rails needing to be 62 feet above the valley floor. The original estimate of December 1896 quoted a cost of £10,000 for a concrete viaduct having eight arches, although according to Ray Stone, this plan was revised "...due to soil conditions." What exactly these "conditions" - perhaps 'difficulties' would be a better word, are not explained. Instead, there may perhaps be an alternative reason why a change of plan took place and which is hidden within the official statement. To explain this we need first to consider the LSWR and the use of concrete for railway viaducts in general. Possibly the first time this material had been fully used was in Scotland, for the Glenfinnan viaduct on the West Highland Line between 1898 - 1901, it remains in use today. Nearer to home, Hockley viaduct on the LSWR line from Shawford Junction to Winchester (Chesil) was built in 1890 / 91 with a concrete core supplemented by conventional brickwork on the exte-

91. *Reported as 'Circa 1900', although unlikely to have been earlier than the start of 1902. The replacement viaduct is seen in place with the earthworks almost complete and in the left distance, topsoil added to the embankment side. The temporary track leading down to the base will be noted. In the distance can just be seen the south portal of West Meon tunnel. Interestingly no reference to the viaduct, in either form, appears in the official railway bridge register. (HCC A04088/2/23)*

rior, the latter seemingly provided purely for aesthetic reasons. Hockley, although devoid of trains, remains to this day, a visual barrier between the M3 motorway and the water meadows of the River Itchen at St. Cross outside Winchester. At the same time as the Meon Valley route was under construction, the Lyme Regis branch was built, including the 10 arch concrete viaduct at Cannington. Inspection of this line, as a prelude to opening, had been scheduled for May 1903, but was abruptly cancelled due to subsidence affecting part of the new viaduct. It was repaired, again in concrete, with a subsidiary arch within an arch and still stands as a monument, although devoid of trains for several decades. No brick facing was provided. All three of the viaducts mentioned were built by different contractors. Did then the LSWR and / or its engineers begin to have second thoughts on the viability of a concrete structure? This would seem a possibility, for as can be seen in No. 90 and inset, work had actually started on the foundations for an 8-arch structure. The view is looking south across the West Meon - East Meon Road, with the south approach embankment raised from chalk excavated from the station site, located just beyond the cutting in the distance. At the time, the northern approach to the viaduct - West Meon tunnel is behind the photographer - appears incomplete. The small contractor's work site at the base will be noted, complete with its raised water tank and hut. The latter cannot be a latrine, not least because of the presence of a chimney, and may well have been the site office. Site latrines were non-existent for the workforce at this time. To complete the story it would have been useful to know when the decision was made to change from a concrete to a metal structure. Certainly it cannot have been as late as May 1903, the structure would never have been finished in time - the line opened in June 1903. Assuming that David Foster-Smith amassed most of his collection before he moved away from Hampshire, it is probably fair to say the excavation scene was recorded sometime before his departure - this was referred to at the start of this work as circa 1902. This would also then fit in with the time that would be taken to design a replacement metal viaduct, have the materials delivered and erect on site. (The accompanying images on the next page showing the metal viaduct are from another collection.) From the above it should not be taken that the LSWR were anti-concrete in any way, such material would feature heavily in LSWR structures in future. Locally too, the station platforms, bridge abutments for the A272 overbridge, some lining of the two tunnels and most importantly, the base supports (five) for the metal viaduct would all be made from concrete. The last named items still visible in 2010. It would be interesting to know what evidence might still exist below the surface as to the footings for the originally planned structure. No details of cost of the actual structure compared with that originally proposed have been discovered.

92. Left - *The great and the good, including the local Parson, Danny Fair, taking the air, on a visit to the site of work at West Meon viaduct. Interestingly the site of the 'up' line would appear complete, that of the down not so. In the event a track was only ever laid on the down side. (HCC A04088/2/24)*

93. Lower left - *The viaduct complete, bridging the road linking West Meon and East Meon, and also the River Meon: the two villages are about 3¼ miles apart. 725 tons of steel were used in its construction, the number of photographs of the structure making it apparent it was a marvel. The length was 77 yards and the spans 51 to 58 feet long. The maximum height was noted by Major Pringle of the Board of Trade as 63½ feet. Ray Stone notes, "When complete, people came from miles around to view it and four locomotives were placed, one on each span, to test the structure and its deflection: several schoolboys among the spectators, who watched until 2.30 pm, were late for afternoon school and were caned." Presumably this was a test arranged by the engineers and LSWR as the official Board of Trade inspection does not refer to the incident. (The official inspection does note, " Solid concrete piers were first proposed, but some weakness in foundations was indicated, and the present type of construction adapted. I could detect no indication of movement in the concrete footings.") On the right is gable end to the roof of what may once have been a contractor's hut.*

96. Opposite bottom - *Included to show the new concrete supports to the piers together with their position. According to the official reports, the line had 21 overbridges, three of the girder type. There were a further 12 underbridges. In addition were 7 culverts with spans from 4' to 10'. Not so well known were the 19 level crossings: four public, six private, and nine occupation. None of these were road level crossings in the commonly deemed phrase. See also No. 107. (KR Collection)*

Three major landowners appear to have been involved in the route taken by the line. The first was Montagu Knight of Chawton House whose land the railway crossed for the first two and half miles south from Butts Junction. Around the area of Privett was Squire Nicholson. His interest extended as far as the south end of Privett tunnel, after which, and certainly as far as West Meon, the name Col. Le Roy Lewis is referred to. West Meon was also the physical mid point of the line, a few miles south of which the strata to be faced by the contractor would also change from chalk to clay.

Peter Swift in some accumulated notes, refers to a slight 'spat' between the LSWR, Col Le Roy Lewis and also involving West Meon Parish Council. It is included as an example of the situation in the locality. "One of the less important, but none the less interesting pieces of information, concerning the construction of the Meon Valley line, is a series of letters written by a Mr. Bircham of the solicitor's office at Waterloo. The content of the letters is a disagreement between the LSWR Company and West Meon Parish Council, concerning a public footpath which the new railway would cross, just to the north of West Meon station. "The letters were written to Col. Le Roy Lewis, who owned the land where the footpath and the railway were to cross, and to A.R. Martin, clerk to the parish council. On studying the two map sections, it can be seen that the point where the line would have crossed the footpath is raised above the ground on an embankment, because of this the council wanted the company to provide a subway. The disagreement arose because the LSWR were most reluctant to provide this subway, no doubt because already a small stream at the

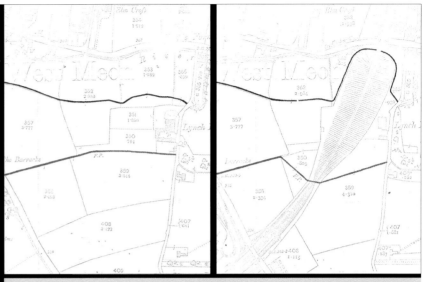

94 and 95. The stream (top line) and footpath (bottom line) seen before and in their final positions. The plan on the right subsequent to the railway being built.

same point had not been provided with a culvert but diverted alongside the base of the embankment, underneath the viaduct and back down the other side of the embankment. When one considers the great expense the company went to in building the line to such a high standard, one wonders why they were so reluctant to provide money for building a subway which would have carried both the steam and the footpath through the embankment? Could it have been that by 1902 the embankment was already built, and constructing a subway would mean excavating through newly deposited chalk spoil, which would be prone to collapse and possibly upset the whole embankment at that point? But, if this were the case why did they not build a brick subway before beginning the embankment? The company put forward three alternative routes for the footpath -

1.) Diverting the path alongside the base of the embankment and back down the other side, as with the stream.
2.) Providing steps up both sides of the embankment.
3.) A slight diversion of the path to the south, at which point the land is at the same level as the railway and thus the path crosses it on the flat.

Viaduct West Meon.

"At first the council were still adamant on a subway, but at a later date they reconsidered, and agreed on the third alternative, which would mean only a small increase in the length of the path. The change of mind was probably due to the company solicitor, Mr. Bircham, via Col. Le Roy Lewis, pointing out that in a similar case in 1897, the House of Lords decided that a railway company whose line crossed a public footpath, was under no obligation to carry the railway over the footpath, or the footpath over the railway by means of a bridge. Not directly concerning the railway, but still of interest, was the cost of erecting a stile and some fencing - I believe at the point where the path diverged from its original course, on the west aide of the railway. Two estimates were received by the parish council from local firms. W. Read & Sons supplied an estimate of £27 10s.while J. Abburrows thought a more realistic cost would be £11. 12s 6d. It is quite obvious which of the two tenders would have been accepted by the council."

This page, *(Nos 97 - 99) Three views from the HCC archive, showing what is reported to be construction at West Meon "Circa 1900". The date may be correct with construction progressing simultaneously at several separate locations. The fact similar images were not available from the DFS album means he may very well have been responsible for overseeing the navvys in just one specific area - although that does not then explain the presence of several views of Wickham later!*

Whatever, if this is West Meon, and it would appear most likely, then what is seen is the initial excavation for the station site, the route of the railway from the approach cutting apparent, with the area being widened and levelled to afford sufficient accommodation for the goods yard and associated sidings and hardstanding.

On images Nos. 97 and 98, it is just possible to make out a line of wooden fencing at the top of the cutting - on the left side. Later, much of the fencing throughout the railway would be replaced by the then standard concrete post and wire. (An excavated concrete fence post near the South Downs Way footpath south of West Meon, displays the date '20 November 1920' on its base, which might well be indicative of an approximate 20 year lifespan for the timber original. At Tisted, immediately adjacent to the surviving metal overbridge at the station, light rail section has been used for fence posts which were still extant in 2005. The immediate conclusion might be this was from the narrow gauge track left over from the construction but it would appear to be of too light a section. In the official bridge list, no number or detail is given for this Tisted bridge, although it was likely to have been No. 15.

The three images display a mix of muscle power, both human and equine and for the first time a tracked steam excavator - see also opposite page. Was the excavator brought in to speed the work, due to the previously referred to shortage of labour, or simply because it was the latest in technology? As with the rail borne example seen at Nos 115,116 & 118, a rudimentary form of weather protection has been added. (The lower view on this page is reproduced to the maximum extent of the print.)
(HCC A04088/1/7)
(HCC A04088/1/5)
(HCC A04088/1/21)

100. Above - *With the 1846 church of St. John the Evangelist, West Meon in the background, the excavations are clearly of interest to the local populace. Using the church as a reference point, it is possible to locate the scene as just north of the station site: the wooden fencing referred to on the opposite page also apparent. (HCC A04088/1/6)*

101. Right *- The excavator referred to and also at least one female visitor. In both this and the view above, members of the public are seen. Deliberately avoiding comparisons with Health & Safety today, this is one of several images where non-navvy / contractor staff are present. (Possibly an appeasement to the disruption caused by the works to the local populace.) Conversely it may also have been simple interest, work of this magnitude never before - or since – having taken place in the Meon Valley. The location is given as West Meon but it is not possible to be more specific as the scene would have changed literally hour by hour. Other than on the excavation of Privett tunnel, we do not know if work continued around the clock, although at this time Sunday was still probably kept as sacred. Two other points are of interest: the first the somewhat battered container - coal fuel for the excavator perhaps, and bearing the designation 'R……..', no doubt 'Relf'. This is also one of the few images where there is a reasonably clear view of the contractors track, the rail of which is spiked directly to the sleepers. The second concerns the excavator itself which is placed on what appears to be an isolated point compared with the trackwork nearby: possibly the same location as seen at No. 105. (HCC A04088/1/22)*

Nos. 102. Top, 103. Bottom, and 104. Opposite page. Three views of the station site at West Meon in varying stages of building. In No. 102 the basic excavation has been completed and material, bricks at least, are on the site ready for, it is believed, the overbridge and station building. (A further pile of stacked material including timber is on hand to the right.) The temporary wooden bridge would have been provided to maintain a public right of way and was suitable for pedestrian use only. In other locations, temporary wooden bridges were similarly provided as necessary. The view is looking north towards the viaduct. Of particular interest is the presence of the two LSWR wagons. From what is clearly an incomplete formation north, these wagons must have arrived from the south and can only confirm that a temporary route was in place accessed from Knowle Junction. In some respects it is surprising the LSWR would have allowed their own wagons to traverse what was clearly a temporary way. In No. 103 work has obviously progressed, as the bridge, No. 34, 40' 8" span with a 41' 4" skew and a clearance to the arch of 15' 4", is now complete. At the time it was known as Winchester Lane Bridge. Work has also progressed beyond, with topsoil added against the chalk although still only a temporary way exists on which are standing at least three contractors wagons. The scene may well have been recorded on a Sunday as no workers appear present. (HCC A04088/4/1 and HCC A04088/4/55)

104. *Workers engaged in construction of the station at West Meon. There is a suggestion that due to delays in completing the route the LSWR brought in their own staff to complete the work but this cannot be confirmed. What we do know is the design of the stations was carried out by Mr. Thomas Phillips Figgis* [1] *of London. The five station buildings were of similar design and located, station to station, on alternate sides of the track. The design at Wickham, Droxford and Privett being a mirror image of that used at West Meon and Tisted. (The reason for this was the positioning of the building relative to the approach access.) This particular style of station building was not used anywhere else on the LSWR. Again the LSWR wagon will be noted: was the view taken at the same time as No. 102? The methods of building construction, scaffolding, planks, hod carriers, water butts, mixing etc, will be familiar to many readers as hardly changing for several subsequent decades. The LSWR wagons have, of course, conventional buffing and drawbar gear, which may explain why at least one of the engines depicted earlier, see No. 38, retains standard buffers. From the dress of the men these would appear to be artisans rather than navvies. Consequently we might ask where they were accommodated during the work as it would be unlikely they would have travelled daily. The image is referred on the HCC website as circa 1905, although this clearly cannot be correct. (HCC A04088/3/9)*

1. According to Wikipedia, T.P Figgis was a British architect who designed a number of other railway station buildings in the London area.

105. Left and **106. Above** - 'Action scenes' at an unreported location. It is interesting the excavator appears to be standing on its own isolated track whilst the raised end to the track under the wagons may have been to reduce collisions - notice the wagons have been chocked. One man would appear to be operating the machine, which may be another example to those already depicted or the same with the weather protection removed.

108. Opposite far right - Possibly a few moments after No. 105 as the full wagon has been removed. As referred to earlier, much of the excavation work on the MV line was undertaken by hand. This is slightly unusual as just a few years earlier mechanical aids had been used to build the neighbouring Basingstoke and Alton line.

107. **Above** - *Mr. Anderson, reported as an Engineer involved in the building of the viaduct at West Meon. He is seen in cycling clothes outside what may be The Rectory at West Meon. (The resident engineer for the line on behalf of the LSWR was Mr. Henry Byers.)*

109. Left. *Construction at an unreported location. Compared with many of the earlier images, this one is clearly a posed view, even the excavator has been turned to maximise the scene. On the machine itself the firehole door is also open, indicating this may have been recorded at the end of the shift. The nipper on the footplate is also seen with oil can in hand. (Did this machine double as a crane as well as an excavator?) Several other nippers are seen on the left, including one with a wagon sprag. At the top of the cutting, the men, together with their equipment cannot be clearly identified - or were they present to remove the top soil by hand for later re use?*

110. Right - *Excavation at an unreported location but one which gives the impression of a deep excavation. Work would have progressed regardless of the weather, but as been mentioned, certain of the years between 1898 and 1903 were reported as having poor weather. (Specific weather reports for these years relative to the local area have not been located.) Compared with the chalk strata found for some 17 miles south of Alton, the final miles were through clay soil and reported as 'most unfavourable for railway construction'.* [1]

1. 'The Railway Magazine' of 1903, pages 499 to 505, in a seven page article reporting on the rationale behind and construction of the new route.

111. This page, top - *Contemporary West Meon. The church will of course be recognised whilst in the right distance (indicated) can be seen the Alton road (A32) climbing steadily up the hill. To its right (indicated) is the chalk of the embankment leading to the cutting at the south end of West Meon tunnel. It was this hill that the railway had to burrow through.*

112. This page, left - *'Snap time' for a navvy group. The location is not confirmed. Whilst similar to, it is not certain if the missionary is David Smith.*

113. Opposite page, left - *What is certainly a different machine to that seen in No. 109 etc. The location not reported but included as south of Droxford due to the heavy loam. Note the water tank as a supply for the excavator (- the latter perhaps even an adapted crane?) on the wagon to the right.*

114. Opposite page, right - *Construction of an overbridge, location not reported.*

115. Left, 116. Above, and **118. Opposite right** - *Excavation through heavy clay. Apart from the contract for the Meon Valley line, Messrs. Relf were also responsible for the doubling of the 'Farnham, Alton and Winchester' line for a distance of 1 mile 3 furlongs and 4½ chains from Alton to Butts Junction, as well the 2 mile 3¾ chain Fareham deviation. In December 1896, these were costed at £15,956 7 s 11d. and £35,329 9s 2d. respectively. It is possible any of these three images may then relate to either the MV line or the Fareham deviation line - the latter incidentally originally costed for just a single line of rails but with all earthworks and bridges etc. built for double track. Notice the very basic turnouts: a number of track components are also visible*

against the cutting side. There are also two horses, nose to nose in the centre, both animals clearly well used to the noise associated with the workings. It is not certain who would have been responsible for laying the temporary track, possibly the men themselves rather than a special 'gang'. (The term 'Ganger' was used in navvy days to indicate the man in charge of gang of navvies. Later the railways would use the same term to indicate a man in charge of a group who maintained the track over a specified distance.)

117. Above - Taking a break from work, the horses are seen with nose bags. Due to the undulating terrain of the route, embankments of
a consistent height for any length were rare. On the basis then of the presence of chalk, it is possible this could be south of Warnford in the vicinity of Corhampton. The horses would have been the property of the contractor Relf, and had probably been employed on other of his works, several of which involved railway building in Devon / Cornwall.

118. Top left - *Bridge building in the Forest of Bere, south of Droxford. This is believed to be bridge No. 59, known as Button's Hill Bridge, a public crossing at Mislingford sidings. Built of a brick arch and abutments, it was 28' wide having a skewed arch width of 39' 10" and with 16' 1" clearance from the trackbed.*

119. Opposite page, top right - *An unreported location, possibly Liberty Road bridge - carrying the present day A32 over the course of the railway south of Mislingford. At this stage of course ballast has still to be added, yet, in its incomplete stage, the view is very similar to that as would appear just over half a century later with the rails torn up and ballast removed.*

120. Bottom left - *Possibly the reverse view from the same spot with the original route of the public road in the foreground.*

121. Opposite page, bottom right - *It must not be forgotten that before the railway could be built, the way had to be cleared. The Forest of Bere between Droxford and Wickham one of the few places where timber might be obtained. Clearing a path was a priority to allow access to West Meon from the south.*

122 and 123. This page, left and right - *At Wickham the railway crossed the River Meon twice, firstly just south of what become the station site and again shortly afterwards, this second time with a three span wrought iron girder bridge. Between the two river crossings were the road overbridges of Asylum Road Bridge (- nowadays more kindly known as Fareham Road) and Bridge Street as well as a continual substantial embankment. From the two illustrations on this page, it would appear as if some form of pile driving is taking place alongside the temporary structure. This wooden trestle allowed access north for contractors materials which would otherwise have needed to be transported by road. In 123, a few miniature fir trees can be seen on the bank, either planted by the men, or perhaps evidence that the bank nearest the photographer was pre-existing? The church in the background is that of St Nicholas, which stands at the crossroads of Bridge Street / Southwick Road and the modern day north - south A32. In consequence this can be used to position the view which must then be the northernmost of the two river crossings. The question over pile driving is that when completed, this northernmost bridge consisted a three spans. South of Wickham, there was another substantial bridge over a wider River Meon at this point, consisting wrought iron girders with trough decking.*

(No 122. Wickham Parish council Stan Woodford.)

124. Top left - Tipping of the embankment just south of the River Meon bridge. The locomotive could well be either No. 11 or 'Annie' - see Nos. 36 & 37.

125. Top right - Believed to be the completed road bridge known as Wickham Church Bridge, referred to at 122 / 123 as Bridge Street. This was Bridge No. 68 at 70 miles 74 chains from Waterloo. 29' 9 " span and a maximum clearance height of 16' 9". Standard practice wrought iron girders, trough decking and brick abutments were provided. The same form of construction was used for Asylum Road Bridge - sic, which was within a few inches of being of identical size. The culvert seen above was No. 67A and of 6' height. It was reported that several cottages in Wickham had to be demolished to accommodate the railway in the vicinity of the Asylum Road Bridge.

126. Left - Almost a final view of a navvy group, seemingly attacking the clay of the 'Reading Beds',

126 - *Work complete - almost, at Droxford. This is looking south, the corner of the station canopy can just be glimpsed top left. Starting on the ground, the final permanent way has been laid and is complete, one wagon of indeterminate type, just visible in the background. On the platforms the timber footbridge is complete, but whilst the down starting signal has been erected clearly the signalling is not finished as there as yet no windows in the signal box. The latter does, however, have its name board. Point rodding has also been added. Before inspection and opening, much in the way of tidying up in the cess, 'four foot' and 'six foot' - meaning on the edges of the track, between the rails and in the gap between the two sets of running rails took place, the official inspection was on 2 and 3 April 1903, consequently this view must predate that time, confirmed as such by what appears to be a winter scene from the trees in the background. The official inspection report was reproduced in Ray Stone's book so need not be repeated here, although suffice to say, no major problems were reported although in view of some of the gradients that existed in the vicinity of the stations, recommendations as to working practices were made which the company, the LSWR, were to instigate. Public opening, however, did not take place until June 1903, and which almost confirms the thought that despite having a new railway complete and available to traffic, there was no apparent urgency to do so. It may have been that non-passenger traffic did predate the public opening, such workings giving experience to the operating department as well as the opportunity to further consolidate the earthworks as well as verify no difficulties arose as a result of the passage of trains.*

127. *The new building at Wickham. This image also appears in Denis Tillman's 'Meon Valley Revisited'[1] volume, together with an explanation as to the 'left and right' handing of the buildings. (See also comment at No. 104.) It is a matter of regret that no images have been located of construction of the various staff cottages at the various stations.*

I. KRB Publications, 2003.

128 Left - *In the cutting between Butts Junction and Alton, work is progressing on the widening for the double track. This cutting had originally been built for the Winchester & Alton railway (Mid Hants Line), and like many others the original bridges, the one seen is Mount Pleasant Road, were to double track width although not so the earthworks.*

129. Centre - *Two contractors locomotives, both 0-6-0ST type and which may either both be Manning Wardle or the one nearest the camera possibly of Hudswell Clark origin. Notice they are not coupled, with a man, the driver perhaps, on the ground attending to something below the footplate. Regretfully it is not possible to identify the nameplates and any attempt at reading these would be pure guesswork. What is seen and is especially interesting, is what appears behind the rear engine: possibly an early container. Under a glass this appears to be of timber so cannot be additional water for the engine. Ahead are railway owned wagons, one LSWR and one GWR (the latter a common user type.) The location is believed to be the embankment on the approach to Butts Junction from Alton.*

130 . Right *- The ground formation is complete at Butts Junction with standard LSWR fittings for the final permanent way to hand ready to be laid.*

ACKNOWLEDGEMENTS
No book of this type would be possible without the valued assistance of those who have undertaken studious research work previously. In addition to those already mentioned in this work, I must acknowledge my gratitude to; David Ballard, Eric Best, Les Burberry, Graham Hatton, Rod Hoyle, Bruce Murray, Christopher Purdie, Ray Stone, Denis and Avril Tillman, Alastair Wilson, Bob Winkworth and of course, David Foster-Smith.